Book Clubbed

K.D. McCrite

Annie's®
AnniesFiction.com

Library of Congress-in-Publication Data
Book Clubbed / by K.D. McCrite
p. cm.
I. Title
                            2017956637

AnniesFiction.com
(800) 282-6643
Amish Inn Mysteries™
Series Creator: Shari Lohner
Series Editor: Jane Haertel
Cover Illustrator: Kelley McMorris

10 11 12 13 14 | Printed in China | 9 8 7 6 5 4 3 2 1

1

The unseasonably warm March wind blustered and swirled behind her as Liz Eckardt practically toppled into the Sweet Everything bakery located next door to her bed-and-breakfast, the Olde Mansion Inn.

"Hang onto your hair!" Naomi Mason called from behind the counter.

Liz laughed and ran her fingers through her mussed shoulder-length blonde hair. "It's a little late for that. The weather forecast for today should have been 'Skirt Alert!'"

Naomi grinned. "I hear we might be getting snow by the weekend, even though it's warm today."

"I've been more than a little worried about that," Liz said as she sat down at one of the small tables. "I have guests coming from Kansas, Louisiana, Florida, and New Hampshire. Bad weather might cause them to cut their plans short."

"Or keep them here longer than anticipated." Naomi, ever optimistic, poured two cups of coffee and brought them to the table. Although the hour was quite early and the bakery hummed with activity, her good friend seemed ready to take a few minutes from the business of waiting on customers to join her for a short break. Naomi's assistant, Candice Woodhouse, brought them some warm doughnuts on a tray and two small plates.

Naomi sat down and took a long drink from her cup. She closed her eyes for a few seconds. "Mmm. First coffee I've had all morning."

"Then it's past time you took a break. Candice is efficient enough to pick up the slack for a bit." Liz bit into the sweet, warm pastry, relishing how it melted in her mouth.

"My staff is great, thank goodness. So, who are all these guests coming in today? What time are they arriving?"

"I don't have an ETA, but I expect they'll be here sometime this morning. They're writers on a 'working retreat.'"

"A working retreat." Naomi laughed. "Now that's an oxymoron if I've ever heard one."

"The fellow who arranged it, Logan Tracy, said serious writers seldom have vacations because they're constantly working inside their heads."

Naomi grimaced. "I wouldn't like that. At the end of the day, I want a warm bath or a cool shower, a nice supper, and then I want to unwind for a while."

"Understandable." Liz sighed wistfully. "And it sounds lovely, but easy days like that don't happen very often at the inn either."

Naomi finished her coffee and refilled their cups. "How many writers are attending this retreat?"

"Only four. They're part of the Master Writers Cooperative, an organization made up of several authors from all over the country. As I understand it, these four met online a few years ago, but have never met face-to-face."

"Meeting someone you've only known online sounds a little scary. Fun, but scary."

"Oh, I think meeting up in real life—or IRL, as the kids say—is happening quite a bit these days. It's amazing how many romances begin online. Or so I hear." Liz nibbled at her doughnut, which was heavenly, still warm and covered in cinnamon sugar.

Naomi frowned. "That's not for me. I don't even like blind dates."

"I have strangers staying in my home all the time. Being an innkeeper has its risks, but I enjoy it."

"You have a knack for it." Naomi smiled. "You mentioned Logan Tracy a minute ago. I've heard of him."

"He's the author of the Detective Jack Todd series."

"That's what I thought. Those books are really popular. You're lucky to have such a famous person staying in your establishment."

Liz gave a little laugh. "It seems so. Sadie is a huge fan. She's so excited."

"I can understand why. Wasn't there a television series based on his characters?"

Liz nodded. "That was several years ago."

"I've read one of his books. Very exciting, but too gritty and bloody for my taste. I can see where they'd appeal to folks who enjoy that kind of story, though. Who else is coming?"

"You've probably heard of Dorn Alexander. She writes romance novels."

Naomi's face lit up, and she set her coffee down. "Oh, sure. I've read quite a few of her books. Nice and clean, funny, a little suspenseful, and a lot romantic. I'd love to meet her. I bet she's really cool. Who else?"

"Francie Sloan."

Naomi was silent for a bit, thinking, then shook her head. "That name doesn't ring a bell."

"I'd never heard of her either, so I looked her up online. Not much info there. A poorly done website and strange little blog. She publishes her own books. They are fantasy stories for adults, with elves and fairies as the main characters."

"That's interesting. Not my preference, but everyone likes to read something different"

"I looked at a free preview of one of her books. And I'm sorry to say I didn't think it was very good." Liz finished her doughnut and wiped her hands on a coral-colored paper napkin.

"So who is author number four?"

"She's young and unpublished. Camille Connor." Liz's cell phone rang. She retrieved it from her purse and glanced at the screen. "It's Sarah," she said to Naomi. "Hello?"

"Liz, can you come home? There's been an accident."

Her heart leaped. Images popped into her mind of injury to Sadie Schwarzentruber or Mary Ann Berne, close friends and owners of the Sew Welcome Shop that was housed in her inn. Or maybe something had happened to Beans, her brown-and-white English bulldog.

"Who's hurt? What kind of accident?"

"Someone has fallen down the staircase, but I don't know who she is." Distress edged Sarah's normally calm voice. "I've already called 911."

"I'll be right there." Naomi gave Liz a worried look as Liz got up and shrugged into her jacket. "Something has happened to someone at the inn."

Naomi jumped to her feet and called to Candice, "I'll be back as soon as I can."

The two of them ran toward the inn, aided by a wind that pushed them forward as if it understood the need to hurry. The sound of sirens filled the air as they burst inside, through the foyer, and into the rotunda. At the bottom of the staircase, Sarah was hunkered on the floor next to a woman sprawled facedown in a widening pool of blood. The woman was thin and blonde, with long arms and legs. She was dressed in what appeared to be a stylish pair of violet trousers and a black blouse, but she wore no shoes. Beans sat nearby, his broad head tilted to one side as if trying to figure out what was going on.

"My goodness!" Naomi gasped. "Who is that?"

Sarah moved out of the way so Liz could take her place. "I don't know. I just came in a couple of minutes ago, and there she was."

"The shop isn't open, so Sadie and Mary Ann aren't here yet," Liz said, glancing toward Sew Welcome. "How did she get in?"

"Sadie and Mary Ann are outside. I saw them by the lake when Isaac dropped me off," Sarah said. Jaynes Lake was a lovely body of water just beyond the backyard. Isaac was Sarah's husband, and the son of Liz's Amish cousin Miriam.

"What are they doing out there?" Naomi said.

Sarah shook her head.

Liz leaned closer to the injured woman, felt for a pulse and found it, faint as a butterfly's whisper. The woman moaned, but did not move.

"Ma'am?" Liz said. "Can you hear me?"

The sound of the siren stopped outside the inn, but more sounded in the distance, coming closer.

"I'll go let them in, then get coffee started," Sarah said.

A few moments later, Chief Stan Houghton strode into the room. In his fifties, the stocky, gray-haired lawman exuded both competence and kindness. Liz trusted him and his police force to take good care of her adopted hometown, Pleasant Creek, Indiana. Beans had resumed his usual position, flat on the floor, but now lifted his head and wagged his stumpy tail. Since he'd come into her ownership, Liz had discovered that the dog was a decent judge of character.

"Good morning, Chief."

"Morning." He paused long enough to give Beans a scratch behind the ears. "I was just a few streets over when a call came in that something had happened here." He cast a quick, efficient look around then went straight to the unconscious woman. He squatted next to her, felt for her pulse. "How did this happen?"

"I wasn't here when she fell. No one was. Sarah's the one who found her."

The sirens stopped. The ambulance had arrived. Stan studied the figure on the floor, a frown etched deeply between his brows. "Who is this woman? One of your guests?"

"I don't know. I don't have anyone checked in yet, but it's likely she's a guest. Or maybe one of the Sew Welcome customers. I can't imagine why anyone else would be here so early."

The chief looked toward the darkened shop, then glanced around the room again. "Where are Sadie and Mary Ann?"

"Sarah said they were down by the lake when she got here, so I assume they are still there. The doors have been unlocked since before seven this morning."

He cut a glance toward Naomi, who had been standing quietly, observing everything.

"Liz was with me. I came with her when Sarah called." Naomi's tone almost sounded defensive, as if she thought the chief didn't believe Liz. Not that Liz could blame him for doing his job.

The paramedics brought in a stretcher and equipment. The wheels rattled across the hard floor, and Liz found the sound both irritating and reassuring. She stepped aside so they could reach the woman.

Mary Ann and Sadie burst in, pink-cheeked and out of breath.

"We heard sirens!" Sadie marched toward the group.

"What happened?" Mary Ann's eyes were as big as dinner plates.

While the paramedics gently rolled the woman over, the chief got his phone out and took several pictures.

"Who is *that*?" Sadie pointed at her.

"We don't know," Liz said. "We were hoping you did."

The chief raised one eyebrow at the women.

Sadie leaned in, gawping at a face that was so broken and bruised, even the stranger's own mother might be hard-pressed to recognize her. "I don't think I know her."

"Neither do I," Mary Ann said faintly. She put one hand to her throat. "What happened?"

Liz shook her head. "Sarah said the woman was lying there when she got here a few minutes ago."

"But she wasn't here when we left for a quick walk down to the lake," Sadie said.

"How long ago was that?" the chief asked.

"Fifteen, maybe twenty minutes."

"Do you often leave the doors unlocked when no one is here?"

"We didn't lock the front door after we got here this morning because Liz or Sarah is always here." Mary Ann looked at Liz. "I assumed you were upstairs, doing something last minute. Or maybe in your quarters, fixing your hair or something."

"You said you thought she might be one of your guests, Liz?" He looked at her. "I don't see a purse nearby, so unless she's got some identification in a pocket somewhere, it might not be easy to figure out who she is."

"I have four guests set to arrive today, but I don't know what any of them looks like." Liz watched, feeling light-headed as the woman was strapped onto the gurney. "Is she going to be all right?"

"It's hard to say, ma'am," one of the paramedics said. "She took quite a tumble." They quickly wheeled her out of the house.

As the ambulance drove away, lights flashing and siren wailing, Sadie said, "I hope she makes it."

"So do I." Liz pulled her phone from her pocket. "I'm calling the three women scheduled to be here today. Surely she's one of them."

But each woman answered her phone and reported she was fine and on the road to Pleasant Creek. Questions roiled in Liz's brain. "I don't understand this. Who is she? Where did she come from? How did she get in the house without anyone knowing about it? How long has she been in here? I mean, if she was at the foot of the stairs so early this morning, maybe she's been hiding out in the inn somewhere."

"You think that's a possibility?" the chief asked.

"Anything is possible I suppose." She shuddered at the notion.

Sarah came into the room with a bucket of water, several rags, a large apron, and some rubber gloves. "I will try to get this cleaned up before anyone else gets here."

"Hold off on that." Without saying more, the chief examined the staircase, step by step, pausing here and there to take photos. At one point he removed a small plastic bag and cotton swab from a pocket and rubbed the swab over blood stains on the stairs. The women exchanged glances with one another.

"Why did he do that?" Mary Ann whispered.

"Maybe he'll send it off for DNA to identify her if she doesn't . . ." Liz swallowed hard and left the rest of the sentence unspoken.

They watched as the chief examined the floor of the landing. Liz craned her neck and saw him study the newel post at the head of the stairs. He took several pictures of it from different angles, then disappeared down the hallway.

"What's he doing up there?" Sadie asked in an undertone.

"I don't know."

"Liz, will you come up here please?" the chief called.

As she went upstairs, the bright splashes of blood on the wall made her queasy. The squared edge of the newel post offered a gruesome image. She looked back down the staircase, and it was easy to see the path the woman had taken on her descent. A cold finger of fear ran down the length of her spine.

"Mind if I look in these rooms?" the chief asked, his hand on the doorknob of the Rose of Sharon Room.

"Go ahead. Maybe there'll be something to identify her in one of them."

He gave her a sharp look. "You didn't look up here already?"

"I haven't had time. As I said, I was at Sweet Everything next door when Sarah called." Once again she related the events. This time instead of just listening, he tapped the information into his phone. She followed him through the guest rooms, looking in every nook and cranny, and finding nothing unusual.

He looked up the stairway that led to the third floor. "Can I look on the third floor too?"

"Of course."

But the search of the Sunrise and Sunset Rooms, and a scrutiny of the first floor, including her private quarters, proved futile as well. By the time they finished, Sadie and Mary Ann were in the quilt shop and Naomi had gone back to the bakery. Sarah was cleaning the blood as placidly as though she were mopping up spilled water. The young woman had an iron stomach and a fearless disposition. Liz thought, as she often did, that she didn't know what she would do without Sarah.

The chief stopped into Sew Welcome for a minute, and then once again they stood near the staircase. "Chief, you've been so meticulous in your examination of the inn. What do you think happened?"

"She came down those stairs, hard."

That much was obvious. The answer frustrated her. "But do you know why? If there is a hazard on the steps, I need to get it repaired as soon as possible."

He shook his head. "I saw no reason for her to fall. There's no obstacle or hazard, like torn carpeting or slippery flooring."

She let this sink in. "Surely she didn't hurl herself down them."

He said nothing.

A disturbing image came into her mind, and she could not shove it away. She hated to ask, but needed to know. "Do you think she was pushed?" The idea was fearsome and ludicrous, and she wanted to reject it immediately.

"It's possible, but you said no one else was in here. Right?"

"As far as I know. Or she might have tripped over her own feet. Or maybe her purse strap got in the way. Of course, we found no purse, and she was barefoot."

"I'll need the names of the guests you're expecting."

"Stan, they aren't even here yet. Do they have to know about this?" She inwardly winced at the near-pleading tone in her voice. "I mean, they are coming for a *retreat*, which should be relaxing, not anxious."

The chief held her gaze. "I understand your concern. I may not have to talk to them at all if she wakes up soon and can tell me what happened. But if this turns out to be something more than an accident, I or one of my men will be around."

She blew out a long breath. "I hope it doesn't come to that."

His smile was understanding, even comforting. "Me too. But now, their names, please."

He tapped in the information she gave him, then turned to Sarah, who was still cleaning the staircase.

"Sarah? Anything else you want to add?"

She stopped working and shot a quick glance at Liz. The Amish community was never comfortable talking with the police.

"It's okay," Liz said. "We're just trying to find out who she is, or where she might have come from."

"But I don't know anything. I came in to work and saw her lying at the foot of the stairs. I called 911, then called Liz on her cell phone."

"Did you hear or see anyone or anything unusual?"

"Not at all."

"Think hard. Anything at all?"

She met his eyes steadily. "Nothing."

"I see." He made a few notes on his phone, then slipped it into his pocket, his features inscrutable. "You'll get in touch if something comes to mind?"

She nodded.

"Liz, you too?"

"Of course."

Liz liked and respected Stan, but when he left the inn a few minutes later after making another stop at Sew Welcome, she breathed a sigh of relief. She hurried into the shop, where Sadie and Mary Ann stood behind the counter, silent and uneasy.

"What did he say to you two?"

"He asked a lot of questions, wanted to know if we'd had any odd customers lately, that sort of thing," Mary Ann said.

"And then he told us that we needed to tell the police anything we could about this mysterious woman," Sadie said, indignant. "As if we would hold something back."

"He's just being thorough," Liz assured her. "That's what makes him a good police chief."

Sadie frowned. "You know what probably happened? She probably walked in to get a room, and when she found no one down here, she went upstairs trying to find you."

"Then she fell when she came back down." Liz nodded. "That makes sense, and I hope you're right."

"But our chief seems to think we all ganged up on her and threw her down."

"Oh, Sadie, you exaggerate. He does not. As I said, he's just being thorough."

"I suppose so. I'll keep telling myself that, anyway. But why didn't she have a purse or shoes?"

"That makes no sense," Liz agreed. She looked at her watch. "I should go to the hospital and check on her."

"You can't do that," Mary Ann said. "You have guests coming."

"But someone needs to find out who she is and let her family know."

"I'll go," Sadie said. "I'll find out all about her. I'll get you a full rundown—"

"You should stay at the shop, Sadie," Mary Ann interrupted. "After all, the Burgess sisters are coming in this morning, and you have a good rapport with them. I'll go to the hospital. No, don't protest, Liz." She held up one hand. "You need to be here for those new folks coming in."

"But Sarah can—"

"Sarah has her hands plenty full cleaning up the mess on your stairs. Your time is best spent here, being the innkeeper. Sadie's just fine in the shop, and I am good at dealing with people at the hospital. And Caitlyn will be there, so I'll find her. All right?" Caitlyn Ross worked at the local hospital as a nurse and was a friend and fellow member of their quilting group, the Material Girls.

Liz considered Mary Ann's words, realized the wisdom of her plan, and nodded. "Okay. But you must let me know whatever you find out."

"I'll do that." She started toward the door, then looked back and said, "Try not to worry, Liz."

"'Worry is like a rocking chair. It gives you something to do, but it doesn't get you anywhere,'" Sadie quoted. "I don't know who said that, but there's a lot of sense in it."

A severely injured stranger, blood on the staircase, and a writers' retreat beginning that day. How could she not worry?

2

Sarah was still cleaning up bloodstains when a petite, middle-aged, dark-eyed woman dressed in fitted black capris and a white silk shirt came into the inn. Her going-gray black hair hung in two braids in front, halfway to her waist. She looked like the illustrations Liz had seen in an old storybook about Heidi of the Alps—if Heidi had been fifty years old.

"Hi!" she said brightly. "I'm Francie Sloan from the Master Writers Cooperative. Is everyone here already?"

Liz shoved down her lingering anxiety and smiled. "Good morning. I'm Liz Eckardt, the innkeeper. It's so nice to meet you." The woman's handshake was limp and chilly, but her smile was friendly. "You are the first one here."

She glanced toward the staircase where Sarah was patting the area dry with some large towels. There were no traces of blood to be seen.

"If you'll register and sign the guest book, Ms. Sloan, I'll help you get settled." Liz led the way to the front desk, where she processed Francie's payment and watched the woman print her name in small, precise letters in the book.

"Please call me Francie. When will the others arrive?" She followed Liz upstairs. She carried a sleek black suitcase that looked as if it had never been used, and a green canvas tote bag that had seen better days. She'd shaken her head adamantly when Liz had offered to help carry them up.

"I'm not sure exactly when they'll get here, but they're on the way. Did the group agree on a time for your first meeting?" Liz asked.

"I think so." Francie's gaze darted around as if looking for something or someone to jump out at her. Her nervous manner made the hair on the back of Liz's neck prickle.

"Well, I trust it won't be a long wait for you." Liz opened the door to the Somewhere in Time Room. "I hope you like this." She stepped back and Francie went inside.

The woman's nervous manner eased a little. "It's beautiful! I love it." She set her suitcase down, but clung to her tote as she gazed at the display of clocks. Most were not running, as the noise disturbed some guests. But one ticked away with a soft rhythm. "I have clocks just like those back home. Lots of them all over the house."

"Do you? Then this will be almost like being at home, won't it?"

"Yes, it will. Oh, and that bedspread is my favorite color. And I love pine floors."

Although the woman had an air of peculiarity, her enthusiasm pleased Liz, who always tried to provide her guests with beauty and comfort during their stay.

She pointed out the bathroom, the linens, the closet, and where the outlets were. "When you're ready, feel free to come downstairs for doughnuts and coffee. You might want to take a walk along the lake, but it's terribly windy. If you do, you'll probably need a jacket and hat."

"All right. Thank you."

Downstairs, Liz sought out Sarah, who was busy putting away clean dishes out of the dishwasher.

"I hope you threw away the gloves and rags you used when you cleaned the stairs," Liz said.

"I did. And I was careful not to get any blood on me and to wash my hands extremely well."

"Good. You can't be too cautious."

The telephone rang, and Liz picked it up.

"It's me," Mary Ann said. "The woman is having emergency surgery to stop internal bleeding. I don't know much more than that. There is a police officer here asking a lot of questions, and I've done my best to overhear what's being said, but I haven't had much luck. Anything new there?"

"One of the writers has shown up, so I'm going to try to play this situation low-key. In fact, I'm not going to mention it unless I have to."

"I think that's for the best. No sense in upsetting anyone unnecessarily."

"Exactly my thoughts."

"I'll talk to Caitlyn soon. She'll be able to keep an eye on things far better than I can. Would you tell Sadie I'll be there before long?"

"I'll let her know. Thanks, Mary Ann."

Liz delivered Mary Ann's message to Sadie in the quilt shop, then went into the sitting room. She was startled to see Francie in an armchair, as silent and unmoving as a corpse, hands clasped atop the green bag in her lap.

"Francie!" Liz laid her hand against her chest, heart pounding. "I didn't hear you come down."

"I decided to wait for the others here, if that's all right with you." She fingered the end of one of her braids. "May I call you Liz?"

"Of course. And you're certainly welcome to wait in here for everyone. May I offer you anything? We have coffee and tea. Or there are soft drinks in the refrigerator, if you prefer something with a little fizz. And don't forget I have fresh doughnuts."

"Thank you, but I'm fine." She glanced at the fireplace. "That makes me think of the fireplace we had when I was a child."

"I think they make a room so cozy, don't you?"

"Very cozy." She played with the ends of her braid and gave Liz an anxious look. "Have you heard from the others yet?"

"Not yet. I'm sure they'll be here directly."

Francie nodded eagerly. "Yes. They will be. Soon, I'm sure."

"Would you rather sit in the four-season room? It has a lovely view of the lake and the grounds."

"No thank you. I'm fine."

"There are books here on the shelf and magazines in the basket."

"I'm fine." Francie seemed perfectly content to sit and do nothing.

What a strange little woman.

In spite of Francie's manner, Liz wanted to be gracious and make her guest feel special. "Tell me about your books."

The woman's eyes lit up and she squirmed like a child. "I write about my experiences and the places I've been."

Liz smiled. "I thought you wrote about fairies and elves."

Francie nodded enthusiastically. "That's right."

Liz sought for an appropriate response.

Francie tipped her head to one side and held tightly to her green bag. "I can tell from your expression you don't believe in fairies and elves or enchanted forests."

"But you do?"

"Absolutely. I've played with the Little Ones since I was a child."

"Have you?" Liz said faintly. She hoped her expression stayed courteous and interested, rather than astonished by the outrageous claim offered with such sincerity.

"An entire family of them lived in the woods behind our house, and when I had to move away, they followed."

"Oh?"

"But I'm not supposed to talk about them." She clamped her lips together and assumed a polite but frozen expression.

Liz sought quickly for a reasonable reply. "I see. Well, I'm sure you enjoy writing your books."

Francie nodded.

"How many have you written?"

She held up eight fingers.

"Did you bring any with you?"

Again, she nodded.

"I need to get back to the front desk. Let me know if you need anything. And I do hope you'll let me buy one of your books, and you'll sign it for me." Liz got up to go.

"Yes! I will." Francie resumed her stolid state and seemed unwilling to move or speak further. Thirty minutes later when Liz peeked in, she still had not moved from her perch in the sitting room.

Liz sat at the front desk, catching up on some bookkeeping, when a handsome, burly older man with gray-sprinkled dark hair came into the inn, pulling a small wheeled suitcase. Dressed in jeans, a chambray shirt, and a dark-brown corduroy jacket, he appeared strong and confident. He paused a few steps inside and slid off his sunglasses.

"Hi, Liz." He spoke as if he had seen her every day of his life and knew her well. But the smile he offered failed to reach his eyes as he came forward, hand extended. "I'm Logan Tracy."

"It's so nice to meet you."

Quick footsteps sounded in the sitting room and Francie Sloan rushed into the foyer toward him, a huge smile wreathing her face.

"Logan! I love your books!" He took a step back as she opened her arms to embrace him. "I am starting a detective series too."

He gave her a small, tired smile. "Francie, I presume?"

She nodded enthusiastically. "I can't wait to talk to you about all my ideas. I've even brought manuscripts that—"

"Hold up. This is a retreat, remember? We're here to write and to share, but I'm not about to be ambushed."

Her smile faltered, and she gazed up at him. "Yes, all right. I'm sorry."

He turned to Liz. "The others haven't arrived?"

"Not yet."

"Then I'll have some time to myself. I assume my room is ready?"

"It is." Liz registered him, then handed him a pen to sign the guest book. A glance toward Francie told her the woman was on the verge of tears. Logan seemed oblivious to her as he scrawled his name across the page.

"Now," he said, putting down the pen, "where's my room?"

Liz took him to the Amish Room. He glanced at the rag rugs on the hardwood floor, the massive but simple walnut bed, the plain decor. "This'll do. Let me know when the others get here." He sat on the edge of the bed and removed his shoes.

Not so much as a thank you.

"Of course. Refreshments are downstairs if you'd like any."

"Not right now." He started to lie down, but paused and looked at Liz. "You want something?"

"No, not at all. I'll be downstairs if you need me."

Clearly a man used to having his own way, he gave her a curt nod and got comfortable on the bed, not bothering to fold back the lovely quilt that covered it. Liz went downstairs, wondering if he would be as brusque and dismissive with the others.

At least he took off his shoes before putting his feet on the bed.

She peeked into the sitting room. Francie had resumed her place, her spine poker-stiff, green bag in her lap and a small notebook in her hand. Her face was tight, and she scribbled rapidly. Liz did not interrupt her and silently retreated from the room, wondering what she'd gotten herself into with something that had seemed so simple.

In the quilt shop, Sadie had laid out several bolts of red cloth, each in a different hue and with a different pattern. She glanced up as Liz walked in.

"For some reason the Burgess sisters always want me to help them. In fact, they call ahead to make an appointment with me. They're polite to Mary Ann, but chilly, as if they don't like her. I don't know why. She's much friendlier than I am. They want red fabric and asked me to have some picked out for them. What do you think of these?"

Liz ran her fingertips over the smooth material. "They are lovely. This one with the subtle bits of deep purple is especially interesting."

"I thought so too. Mary Ann says it looks like someone's pen leaked ink, but I disagree." She lowered her voice. "So I caught a glimpse of Logan Tracy, in person. My heart fluttered like a schoolgirl's. I wanted to go out there and introduce myself, but I didn't want to bother him."

"It's just as well that you didn't."

Sadie's eyebrows went up. "Oh?"

"I think he's tired."

Sadie glanced at her watch. "It's not even ten o'clock yet."

"He's lying down."

"Huh! Well, maybe he drove straight through."

"Straight through from Jacksonville, Florida? That would be quite a drive."

"Yes, but it would explain why he's tired. He's not a young man." Sadie sighed. "Even so, he's as handsome as Sean Connery."

Mary Ann came into the shop, her silvery hair in uncharacteristic disarray. "That wind has changed direction and is blowing up something cold," she said, shivering a bit.

"Snow." Sadie looked unhappy at the prospect.

"Maybe. All I know is the temperature has dropped since I went to the hospital."

"There's always hot coffee, as you know," Liz said, "but before you go to get it, tell us what you know about the injured woman."

"Not much more than I told you when I called. Caitlyn promised to find out as much as she can and will let us know at her earliest opportunity. Liz, are you sure that poor woman is not one of the writers you were expecting?"

"I'm positive. You were here when I talked to all the women on the phone, and they're fine." She turned her head, listening, then said, "In fact, someone has just arrived. Maybe it's one of them."

She left the quilt shop just as a pretty young woman walked into the foyer. Her shiny auburn hair fell in thick waves past her shoulders.

"Hello," Liz said as she approached. "You must be Camille."

The girl gave her a toothy smile and a warm handshake. Her green eyes sparkled. "I am. And you're Liz, the owner of this inn, I'd bet."

"You'd win that bet. Did you have a good trip to Pleasant Creek?"

Camille nodded. "I've been driving around town a bit. It's so pretty here."

"Thank you. I love—"

"Camille!" Francie charged across the floor, the green bag hanging around her neck by its strap like a gigantic necklace. She flung both arms around the girl. "I'd know you anywhere. You're so pretty, just like your photo."

Camille returned the hug with far less enthusiasm. "And I'd know you anywhere, Francie. Those braids are a dead giveaway."

"I've had them since I was a girl, but guess what? I've been thinking about coloring my hair dark red."

"You have?"

Francie nodded like an eager child. "Just like yours."

"I've always liked brunette hair." Camille laughed. "Isn't that the way it is? We always want what we don't have."

Francie played with the end of one braid. "You're right. Maybe I won't color it."

Camille looked around. "Is anyone else from the group here yet?"

"Logan's here." Francie pointed toward the staircase. "He went up and stayed there."

"Oh." Disappointment slipped across Camille's smooth features, then she smiled. "Well, I'll get to meet him sooner or later. And Dorn too. I can hardly wait."

Liz led her to the reception desk, and the young woman signed the guest book in a loopy, backhanded slant. She ran her fingertip over Logan's signature, then laid down the pen and looked around as if familiarizing herself with the surroundings.

"Would you like me to take you to your room?" Liz asked.

"Yes, thank you. I want to look over the short story I finished before I share it with the others at our first feedback session."

Francie started to trail after them, but stopped halfway up the staircase. "I'll just stay here, in case Dorn shows up while you're up there."

"That's a good idea." Camille's voice carried a hint of relief. As they went up the steps, Camille slowed and surveyed the stairs. What was she looking at? She stopped at the landing and stared at the newel post, then glanced around as if she was searching for something hidden. Did she know about the accident?

"Something catch your eye?" Liz asked.

Camille shook her head. "Just looking at the lovely old woodwork. I might write about a place like this someday."

In the Rose of Sharon Room, Camille admired the white vintage furniture and soft, floral decor. "Are these old books first editions?"

"I'm not sure. But they are old."

Camille eagerly took a copy of *Freckles* off the shelf. "My grandmother absolutely loved Gene Stratton-Porter."

"Feel free to enjoy the books while you're here."

"I doubt I'll have much time for reading." She replaced the book and turned to Liz. "Most of my time will be taken up with writing and talking with Logan and Dorn. They have been my mentors."

"How lovely that you can finally meet them face-to-face."

Camille nodded eagerly. "I can hardly wait!"

"If you change your mind, or find that you have time to read, there are more books downstairs, as well as refreshments. Is there anything I can do for you before I go?"

Camille smiled. "No thanks. I'll get settled in and do some writing until Dorn arrives or Logan comes out of his room."

Apparently visiting with Francie was not an option she was considering.

Downstairs in the sitting room, Liz offered Francie tea, but again the woman refused. "I'll wait."

"All right. Is there anything I can get for you while you wait?"

Francie shook her head and cradled the large green bag in her arms.

"If you change your mind, let Sarah or me know."

Francie nodded but said nothing. Liz went into the foyer where the young woman was dusting the reception desk.

"Sarah," she said quietly, "I'm going to the hospital to see if I can find out anything about that injured woman."

"Didn't Mrs. Berne just return from there?"

"Yes, a little while ago, but I can't stand not seeing for myself. The woman was injured in my home, and I have a duty to find out as much as I can and do something if possible."

"Do something?"

"Ask questions. Try to see her. I can't just let her lie there while I do nothing to help."

"Of course not. I'll take care of the new guest if she arrives while you're gone. She'll be in the Heirloom Room, yes?"

"Right. I'll be back as quickly as possible."

3

The nearby hospital lacked the shine and polish of big-city medical centers, but the plain structure offered hardworking teams, modern equipment, and good care to anyone who came through its doors.

Liz parked and hurried inside. She spotted Caitlyn's vibrantly colored hair right away. The slender young woman stood near the nurse's station on the second floor, looking at information on a computer tablet. She glanced up as Liz approached.

"Hi there, Liz!" She smiled. "I was just getting ready to take my break and call you. I would have gotten in touch earlier, but we've been really busy today."

"I understand, and I'm sure that's nothing new."

"Pretty much par for the course in a hospital, even a small one like ours. Would you like to go to the cafeteria and get a cup of coffee?"

"That would be fine."

A few minutes later, they sat across from each other at a small table.

"I'm sure you are here to find out something about that poor woman who fell at the inn, aren't you?" Caitlyn stirred cream into her coffee.

Liz scooted forward on her chair. "Yes. Mary Ann didn't have much information."

"Right. Well, I'll tell you what I know, which is very little unfortunately. She's out of surgery and in recovery, but I don't know her condition at this point. Making it through the surgery is a good sign, though. We've got her listed as Jane Doe, because there was nothing on her person or in her clothes to identify her. Her face is so swollen and bruised that sharing a photo with the public in an effort to ID her would be futile." She lowered her voice. "And here's something else. It looks as if her hair has been chopped off."

Liz frowned. "Chopped off?"

"Right. Not styled, not trimmed, not cut. More like someone took fistfuls of it and whacked it off."

"Like with a knife?" Liz hadn't noticed that.

"Exactly."

Liz shuddered. "Creepy."

"Yes, it is. But that's not all." Caitlyn passed a glance around the cafeteria and leaned closer. "She did not simply fall."

"No?"

"She was pushed."

Liz stared at her. "How do you know that?"

"She said so."

"When? Wasn't she unconscious when they brought her in?"

"She came to for a few seconds, mumbled something that sounded like 'pushed me,' and faded out again."

"That's hardly definitive. 'Sounded like' means she mumbled something, but it doesn't mean she actually said it."

Caitlyn lowered her voice to a whisper. "The doctor found bruises that weren't caused by a fall. Bruises that appeared to be made by hands." She demonstrated by shoving both hands toward Liz, then leaned forward, an entreaty in her eyes. "There are hospital regulations, even in cases of unknown patients, and you are one of the few people for whom I'd break the confidentiality rule. So please, don't let on that I told you anything."

"Of course. I won't say a word to anyone. I appreciate you telling me this, Caitlyn. If it means someone else was in the inn and might be back, then I need to be aware of the situation."

"You are so right." She sipped her coffee and met Liz's eyes. "Do you have any idea who might have pushed her?"

"I don't have a clue. There was no one there when I left to go to the bakery. I'm sure I would have known if there had been."

Even as she said the words, though, she wondered. Maybe someone *had* been there, hiding, lurking, waiting . . . She shuddered again.

"Mary Ann said she and Sadie took a walk after they got to the inn."

Liz nodded. "Sarah had not yet arrived when I left, so this woman simply walked in. And so did the person who pushed her."

Ugly scenarios of attacks raced through Liz's imagination. Who and where was the culprit? Why had it happened? Were her other guests at risk?

"Do the police know that she said she was pushed?"

"Of course. The police are always informed in cases like this one. An officer showed up and asked a bunch of questions, but we don't know anything except that she was attacked. At this point, we can't do much but hope and pray she wakes up."

"I'll certainly be doing that until she pulls through and recovers fully."

"Me too." Caitlyn glanced at the clock. "My breaks always end too soon." She walked with Liz to the exit and said, "I'll let you know if I find out anything more."

"I appreciate that."

She threw a glance behind them and then turned back and whispered, "Remember to keep what I've told you to yourself."

"I'll remember. Thanks."

Liz left the hospital, her stomach tense and her mind uneasy. Who had been in the Olde Mansion Inn with a heart dark enough to push someone down a staircase? The question plagued her as she stopped at the supermarket and picked up a few groceries before heading home.

Mary Ann called out to Liz the moment she came through the rotunda after putting away the groceries.

"I have a message for you." She stood in the door of the quilt shop. Behind her, two heavyset, older women stood with Sadie, critically examining the red cloth she'd laid out that morning. "Logan went out for a sandwich, but he popped in to ask where you were and which room you've designated for their meeting this afternoon. I suggested he ask Sarah, but when he did she said it would be up to you. He asked you to let him and the others know."

"All right. I'll talk to him when he gets back. Did Camille and Francie go with him?"

"They wanted something more substantial, so I suggested Mama's Home Cooking."

"Has Dorn Alexander shown up?"

"Not yet, and the other three seem a little worried about her. Their meeting is scheduled to begin at two o'clock."

"It's already after noon. I'll call her again." She drew her cell phone from her pocket. "She might have had car trouble."

"Wouldn't she have called?"

"Maybe," Liz said. "It could be she's not the type to check in."

"Personally, I don't like to let people worry."

Liz smiled at her. "Dorn Alexander might not be as thoughtful as you are, Mary Ann."

"Most of the characters in her books care about one another and are so kind, so it seems reasonable that she would be. But who knows what she is like personally?"

Liz held up one finger to halt Mary Ann's words when Dorn answered.

"Hi, Dorn. It's Liz Eckardt again. I'm checking in with you to see if you're—"

"An engine light in my car came on, so I stopped to have it checked out. I'll be there soon."

"All right. I'll let the others know. They were getting worr—"

"I said I'll be there soon." There was a click as the call ended.

Liz was taken aback at the harsh tone and sudden end to the conversation. But maybe the woman didn't like talking on the phone as she drove.

"Just as I thought," she said as she slid her phone into her pocket. "Car trouble. She's on her way, though."

"I hope it wasn't anything major." Mary Ann grimaced. "Cars can be so annoying. Sometimes I think the Amish have the right idea, but then I remember horses have minds of their own and can be every bit as tricky as cars. Anyway, what's the latest news about the injured woman? Any changes since I was there?"

Liz opened her mouth to share what Caitlyn had told her, then caught herself. It was so easy to pour out her heart to this good friend that she had nearly forgotten her promise.

"She came through surgery all right, but that's about all I know at this point. Caitlyn promises to keep an eye on her and keep us updated."

"I hope we get good news soon."

"So do I."

Liz started to turn away, then paused.

"Why were you and Sadie out walking this morning, if you don't mind my asking? That's not your usual routine."

Mary Ann looked uncomfortable and shot a glance behind her at the three women who continued to discuss the bolts of fabric. She beckoned Liz to follow as she moved several feet from the door and spoke quietly.

"It's nothing, really, but I dislike dealing with the Burgess sisters."

"You do? Why?"

She glanced toward the door and lowered her voice. "They are very . . . thrifty. They often purchase old clothes at secondhand stores and rummage sales, then cut them up for quilt pieces."

"That's interesting. But isn't that how quilt making got its start, from worn-out clothes?"

"Sort of. When blankets wore out, they were patched from other worn-out blankets or clothes. Hence the term 'patchwork.'" Mary Ann looked a little abashed. "Actually, it's a good use of resources, and I'm not complaining about it. Back then, scraps were used out of necessity, not art."

"You weren't complaining. You are simply looking out for your business, and that's perfectly understandable."

"Thank you for saying so. But what I find so irksome is that these ladies want to negotiate absolutely everything, trying to buy below cost. Even needles and thread! Sadie doesn't get as frustrated as I do, and she is more willing than I am to indulge in the haggling, which can go on and on. They have been here for over an hour already." She shook her head. "Sometimes, the quilt shop ends up getting the short end of the stick when it comes to those two. I'm convinced losing their business wouldn't be such a bad thing, but Sadie believes we need to remain in their good graces."

She shot a glance toward the shop door, and a small flicker of impatience shot across her face.

"Knowing those two were coming in today, Sadie and I got a little testy with each other almost before we said 'good morning.' We decided to take a walk in this brisk March wind to help blow away the irritation and help clear our heads so we could discuss the matter without snapping at each other. Amazing how fresh air and a lovely view can soothe an uneasy mind. And keep two friends from a heated quarrel."

"Then I'm glad you chose to take that stroll. But I wish I knew who got into the house and when."

"Well, that woman in the hospital is who got into the house. The question remains, when did she arrive?" She narrowed her eyes and studied Liz's face. "You don't think someone else was here too, do you?"

Liz caught herself again before she blurted out what Caitlyn had shared. She wanted to bite her tongue hard to help remind her. Better to find something else to do than stand and chat with Mary Ann. Sooner or later, confidential information was bound to slip out with such a good friend and listener. She almost wished Caitlyn had said nothing.

"I meant that we don't know who she is, so we don't really know who was here. Excuse me, but I need to talk with Sarah then make a phone call. And have some lunch." She tipped her head toward the quilt shop. "Good luck with them."

"Gee, thanks," Mary Ann said unhappily. "I guess there's some inventory I can rearrange until they leave."

"Or maybe you'll get some other customers."

Mary Ann brightened. "Now that's a good thought."

Sarah had finished upstairs and was now in the utility room, the scent of clean cotton rising on steam that misted up from the iron as she ironed household linens.

"Did Logan mention a preference for rooms in which to have their meeting this afternoon?"

"No, he just asked which room they could use. There's potato chowder on the stove, and it should be ready to eat. The weather is turning cold. That soup will warm you."

"That sounds wonderful, Sarah. I'll have a bowl of it as soon as I make a phone call."

Sarah turned back to the snow-white tablecloth, and the iron hissed as she smoothed out the wrinkles. Liz started to leave the room, but paused and said, "There is something beautifully comforting about freshly ironed linens. I appreciate you taking the trouble."

Sarah's glance held a trace of surprise. In her community, something as mundane as household chores were as normal and necessary as breathing. Expressed gratitude was not expected, as one certainly did not thank another for breathing. Liz understood, but she believed in letting someone know they were appreciated. She gave Sarah a smile before leaving.

In her quarters a minute later, she called the police station and asked to speak to Chief Houghton.

"Hi, Liz," he said. "You have some information for me?"

"I wish I did, but no. I was wondering if you took fingerprints and a blood sample from that unknown woman."

There was a brief silence, then he replied, "We're running her fingerprints through the database, but if she doesn't have a record, it won't help."

"What about a DNA analysis?"

"Liz, again, if there's nothing to compare it to, her DNA isn't going to help. And we are a small police department."

Liz sighed in frustration. "Sorry, Stan. I know all that. I'm just concerned."

"Of course you are. Let me know if you hear, see, or find anything that will help us. Since I know there's no point telling you to stay out of it."

"None whatsoever, Chief. Thanks for talking to me."

She ended the call and perched on the edge of her small sofa, staring at the floor. Dissatisfaction gnawed at her, but she hardly knew what, if any, steps she could take. The investigation was in the hands of the Pleasant Creek Police Department. She needed to trust them to do their job, as they had done in times past.

There was a soft knock on her door. She opened it to find Sarah on the other side.

"Excuse me for interrupting your private time, Liz, but our guest was asking for you. I sent him to the four-season room to wait for you."

She found Logan standing at the big bank of windows, gazing toward the lake. His laptop sat open on a nearby table. Beyond him, she could see tree branches waving in the wind. In the changeable spring weather, the sky had lost its sunshine, and clouds now scudded across its expanse.

"Hello, Logan. Sarah said you were looking for me."

He glanced at her over his shoulder. "A nice little view you have here."

"I can't take any credit for nature, of course, but thank you." She went to stand beside him. "Everyone seems to enjoy it. Feel free to walk along the lakeshore or sit in the gazebo anytime you like. Although from the look of it, I believe we're in for some inclement weather pretty soon."

"I might take you up on that suggestion. I enjoy being near the water. It's invigorating." He gazed out the window again. "Of course, your little lake is nothing compared to the Atlantic Ocean or even the Great Lakes. They are quite spectacular. Still, what you have out there is nice enough."

She ignored the slight condescension in his tone and manner. "I understand you have a question about where to hold your meetings?"

At her words, he turned from the view. "Much of our time during this retreat will be taken up alone, writing."

"Of course. That's the purpose of a writing retreat, isn't it?"

He gave her a small smile. "It is. Our plan is to come together twice a day. In the afternoons, we will be reading from our manuscripts, then discussing and critiquing one another's work. We will meet again in the evenings to relax and socialize. I hope you'll allow us to meet either here or in the sitting room."

"Certainly. I have no other guests booked for this weekend, so I'll leave it up to you four to choose which room you would rather use. Both rooms have advantages. This one has the view, and the other has coziness and the fireplace."

"Do you have guests who show up without making reservations?"

"We do have people come in quite frequently, looking for a vacancy. More during the tourist season than right now, though."

"We absolutely do *not* want to be interrupted or disturbed during our afternoon sessions." He looked around the room as if expecting unwelcome visitors to come crawling out of the woodwork.

"I understand, but I have no reason to believe it will be a concern."

"Let's hope not. I'll depend on you to keep them away from us."

The sound of voices and rapidly approaching footsteps curbed further discussion and stopped Liz from making a sharp reply. Camille and Francie came into the room. Both women were flushed and breathless, and brought the fresh scent of the outdoors with them.

"That wind is blowing hard," Liz said with a smile. "You look chilled. If you want to sit down, I'll bring you some hot tea or coffee."

"That would be nice," Francie said.

"I don't want nice hot tea or coffee. I want answers." Camille's harsh words took Liz by surprise. Her clear green eyes were as cold and hard as emeralds. "What happened to that guest this morning? Are we in danger?"

"Yes, are we?" Francie chimed in, unsmiling.

"What's all this?" Logan shifted his gaze from Camille to Liz. "Danger from what?"

"Oh, she didn't tell you either?" Camille said. She glared at Liz. "Convenient."

"Tell me what?"

"Francie and I decided to take a little walk around town, and we stopped to have lunch at Mama's Home Cooking. There was someone talking about a woman being hurt here at the Olde Mansion Inn this morning."

Trust local gossip circles to spread the news. How in the world had anyone found out already? There was the confidentiality rule at the hospital, and the police were always close-mouthed about investigations.

Logan's dark eyebrows drew together. "Liz?"

She gave them a look of apology. "I am so sorry that you had to find out that way. I didn't want to mention the incident because I didn't want any of you to worry."

"So it's true?" Camille said.

If she could keep her responses simple and low-key, maybe she could thwart their anxiety. "Someone did fall down the staircase early this morning."

Camille huffed. "Sounds like your stairs are hazardous."

"Actually, we have checked carefully for any loose boards or slippery places and found nothing. It was simply an accident."

"Who's 'we'?" Logan pinned her with his hard gaze. For a moment, Liz felt as if she were about to be interrogated by his fictional detective, Jack Todd.

"The police chief and me."

Francie's eyes got big, and she nearly choked. "You called the police?"

"We called 911 for an ambulance, and the police came because they follow through on every emergency."

"Oh." She toyed with one of her braids.

Liz passed a gaze to each one. "Just be careful going up and down the stairs."

"Maybe someone tripped over that dog." Camille pointed at Beans snoring nearby.

"Don't worry about Beans. He hardly stirs from his favorite sleeping spots, and none of them is upstairs or on the steps. I'm not sure he can even get up the stairs."

Logan gave the dog a smile, then sobered. "So that's it? Someone fell?" His sharp-eyed gaze burrowed into Liz again and he shook his head. "There's more to it than a simple tumble down that staircase, isn't there?"

She winced inwardly, feeling as though he probed her thoughts. "It's just we don't know who this woman is. She had no identification, and since she was unconscious she couldn't tell us."

"Was it Dorn?" Francie gasped. "Maybe it was Dorn. She's not here. Where *is* she?" She grabbed Logan's arm and tugged on it. "*Where is Dorn?*"

Scowling, he shook her off. "How would I know? Liz, do you think the unknown guest is Dorn Alexander?"

"No, I've called her. She had a little car trouble along the way, but she's on the road."

"So you're saying this was just some random person who wandered in off the street?" Camille asked.

"It would seem so, yes." Why couldn't she think of a way to tell them this without sounding like a slipshod innkeeper?

The girl looked less annoyed and more perplexed. "But didn't she register or anything?"

Liz suppressed a sigh, knowing she could not keep everything from people who made their living gleaning information to weave into books.

"Unfortunately, she came while everyone was out. I'm sure she's someone who wanted lodging, and when she found no one down here, she went upstairs to look for us."

"You leave the doors unlocked when no one is here?" Logan asked.

"The Sew Welcome Shop is open, so yes."

"This makes me very uncomfortable." Francie plucked at the ends of a braid with one hand and held the green tote bag close to her chest. "I'm frightened. What if—"

Logan put up one hand in a shushing gesture. "Does this happen often, Liz?"

"You mean someone coming in when no one is around? No, but the inn is open during business hours. As I said, there's usually someone here. This was a simple lapse in communication."

"Maybe we should go elsewhere," Camille said. "What do you think, Logan?"

He stroked his jaw as the other two women looked at him and waited for his response.

"Well, actually, I've stayed in far worse places with far less security, and I've been perfectly fine. I see no reason why this little incident should cause us any hesitation."

"Exactly!" Francie said. "We are perfectly safe here."

"Then the retreat continues?" Camille asked.

He gave a sharp nod. "I hardly think we're endangering anyone— unless our presence disrupts the sleep of yon reclining canine." He made a sweeping gesture toward Beans and struck a dramatic pose.

Liz was relieved when everyone laughed. At least she wouldn't be losing any business over the unfortunate accident.

For now, at least.

4

Shortly before two o'clock, an older, rather unkempt and weathered woman entered the inn. She wore a ratty zebra-striped coat and relied heavily on a cane as she approached Liz.

Shoving back a lock of long, brassy-blonde hair, she said, "I am Dorn Alexander."

Liz gave her a smile. "It's so nice to meet you. I'm Liz Eckardt. Welcome to the Olde Mansion Inn. We've been worried about you."

The woman lifted one brow and leaned on her cane with both hands. "Have you? I can't imagine why. We've been in touch by phone twice today, and I explained I was having car trouble."

"It's just that your first meeting is starting in the four-season room and the other writers have been eager to meet you."

Dorn's heavily made-up face relaxed. "Have they? How lovely. Please take me to them." She handed over her car keys. "My luggage is the trunk. A red Buick."

Most guests brought in their own suitcases and bags, but Dorn obviously had a physical disability. Liz took the keys from her without pause.

"Come this way."

When they entered the four-season room, the other three stopped speaking. Liz introduced them to one another, and they all stared wordlessly at Dorn.

Logan got to his feet and extended his hand. "It's good to meet you in person, Dorn. An honor." His gracious manner surprised Liz. Surely his previous aloofness was due to fatigue, as she'd thought earlier.

"And you as well," Dorn replied. "I admire your writing." She turned to Camille, who had risen from the sofa and approached. "And I recognize those eyes and that auburn hair. How are you, Camille?"

"I'm fine, but it looks as if you—"

"Dorn!" Francie nearly knocked the woman off her feet with an exuberant embrace.

Logan caught the older woman just before she fell. He frowned at Francie. "Try to control yourself, will you? Here, Dorn, sit down. Let me help you." He guided her to the sofa and she sank down a bit awkwardly.

"Did you have an accident?" Camille asked as she returned to her seat.

"Did you?" Francie echoed. She grabbed up her green bag as if it were a lost treasure she'd just found.

Dorn brushed her hair back and gave both women a curious look. "No. Why do you ask?"

"For one thing, Liz told us you'd had car problems on your way here today. And for another . . . that." Camille dipped her head toward the cane now resting across the woman's chair.

Dorn looked at it as if it were so much a part of her that she had forgotten about it. "I've used this thing for years."

"You never mentioned it," Logan said.

She gave him a warm smile. "There was never a reason to."

"I use a walking stick too, sometimes," Francie said.

"You do?" Camille's perfectly shaped eyebrows rose.

"Sometimes."

"Do you have osteoarthritis too?" Dorn asked.

Francie looked confused, but nodded hesitantly.

"I'm sorry to hear that," Dorn murmured. "It can get in the way sometimes." She turned to Logan. "So what's on the agenda today?"

"That's what we've been discussing. We're going to meet every day to share from our newest works in progress, offer critiques, brainstorm plot or character development, or whatever anyone needs help with. Evenings are devoted to relaxing and having fun, but if you'd rather stay in your room and write, feel free to do so."

"But socializing is fun, isn't it?" Francie glanced around eagerly, nodding with enthusiasm.

"In small doses," Logan rumbled. "I'm not much of a people person."

"Neither am I," Francie whispered, leaning in.

"I enjoy parties," Camille said. "Especially after working alone all day."

"Oh me too! Nothing is as good as a party." Francie beamed at her.

A look of annoyance skittered across Logan's face, but he quashed it and turned to Liz. "We'd like you to join us. That is, if Dorn approves. We were talking about it just before she arrived."

"Me? I'm not a writer."

"No, but you're a reader, aren't you?" Camille said. "You have quite a selection of books in your inn."

"Yes, I'm an avid reader when I have time for it. And I love having full bookshelves."

"Then you qualify to be in our meeting. Readers are the ones we writers want to please," Logan said, holding her gaze.

"Readers are so important." Francie's smile was so broad it looked pasted on.

"I think it's a fine idea to have Liz sit in on our critique sessions," Dorn said. "Perhaps she can give us a new perspective."

Liz was both flattered and ambivalent. "But I know nothing about writing, or what makes it good or how stories are put together."

Logan's dark eyes pinned her in place. "But you know what you like when you read it, don't you? That's all that's needed for you to be a part of us."

"That's it. One hundred percent all." Francie sent him a quick look begging for approval.

He ignored her and opened his laptop. "So, did everyone bring a manuscript?"

Sarah came into the room bearing a tray with cups, cream, and sugar for coffee and tea.

While Francie and Camille opened their laptops, Dorn shifted in her chair. "Mine is in printed form, in my attaché case. Liz, would you fetch it for me after you take my luggage to my room?"

"I'll take care of it, Liz," Sarah said in her usual quiet voice.

"Thank you." Liz smiled at her as she handed over the keys. "The red Buick."

"Who goes first?" Francie said, grinning. "May I begin reading my story right now?"

"Let's be fair. Equal time for everyone." Logan did not look at Francie as he tapped a couple of keys. "No one reads until Dorn has her manuscript in hand."

"Yes, of course." Francie sat back stiffly, but she wore her impatience like a bright cloak. She tapped one foot and played with the strap of her bag while she watched the doorway for Sarah to return with the briefcase.

"You're such an eager beaver that you may go first once we start." Dorn's voice had a patronizing quality to it.

Francie's smile brimmed with gratitude. "Thank you so much! I hope you like it. I worked and worked on it, and then I worried that none of you might like it, so I started over twice, and then I—"

"Please don't wear yourself out," Camille said. "It'll be fine."

"Okay." She slouched in her chair and stared down at her screen. The other three exchanged glances. Liz frowned. Thank goodness Francie was still staring at her screen and did not notice their expressions. Liz wondered how these three, who were obviously at different stages of their careers, had come together.

"Here you are." Sarah brought a battered leather briefcase to Dorn, who took it without a word of thanks or acknowledgement.

"Thank you, Sarah," Liz said for the writer. "I think we're all set." Sarah nodded and left.

"May I read now?" Francie looked up.

"Hold your horses." Dorn made a big show of taking out a thick file folder of typed pages and a fountain pen. "My favorite pen. I don't leave home without it." This brought chuckles from Camille and Logan. Francie's grin trembled on her lips.

Dorn took her time putting the briefcase on the floor and shuffling the messy pile of papers into a semblance of order while Francie fidgeted. Liz wondered if Dorn prolonged her actions just to torture the eager woman. At last, she put the folder on her lap, placed the pen on top, folded her hands over it all, and looked at Francie.

Francie sat staring straight ahead, as silent and unmoving as a mannequin. No one said anything for a little bit as they waited for her.

"Well?" Logan's voice was so sudden and sharp they all jumped. "Aren't you going to read?"

Francie turned to him with a bright smile. She cleared her throat, smoothed both braids, and sat up straight, like a child asked to recite in class.

"I named it The Beautiful Valley of the Shining Sun." Once again the others exchanged glances. Dorn shook her head, and Camille rolled her eyes.

"Once upon a time in a beautiful land full of beauty," Francie read, "the lovely bright yellow sun shone on a pretty valley of incredible loveliness, more beautiful than anywhere on earth."

As little as she knew about writing, Liz cringed. Francie's book seemed to be off to a bad start. The other three shifted in their seats. By the time she'd finished reading, thirty minutes had passed and everyone was uncomfortable. No one said anything for a bit as Francie looked at them eagerly.

"You've put in a lot of time, haven't you?" Liz asked the only thing she could think of.

"Oh, not as much as you might think. Once I get started, it flows from me and I write it all down as fast as I can so I don't lose a word of it."

"That much is obvious," Logan said.

"Is it? Oh, good!"

"I get the feeling the setting is beautiful," Dorn said. Francie seemed to be the only one who missed the barely hidden smirk. Liz felt a pang.

"It is so beautiful there," Francie said. "You should see it."

"It's too wordy," Logan said bluntly.

She turned to him. "What do you mean?"

"I mean, you've used a bushel basket of words when a thimbleful will do."

She frowned, shaking her head. "I don't understand."

Camille leaned forward. "Francie," she softened her expression with a smile, "just write what is needed and don't embellish it so much."

Maybe Camille was kinder than her two colleagues. Liz hoped so. In spite of Camille's softer words, Francie looked crushed and confused. She reached for her green bag and held it close.

"You mean fewer descriptions?" Liz asked, trying to clarify for Francie's sake.

"Yes. Tell it straight." Logan pointed to Francie's laptop. "Start over."

"Right now?"

He looked away for a bit and tapped his foot. "No, not right now. Right now, we're doing the critique session." He glanced at her. "Of course, if you wish to work on it now rather than be here, you are free to go. That's up to you."

Camille and Dorn looked at her hopefully, but Francie said nothing else and made no move to go.

"I'll read next," Dorn said. She passed a glance to each one. "I have decided to take a new direction with my writing."

"Oh? Sounds intriguing," Logan said. "In what direction are you going?"

She curled her lips slightly, Mona Lisa–like. "I'm moving away from the same old humdrum romance novels."

"Since when?" Camille asked. "You've never mentioned a word about changing genres in any of our group discussions."

Dorn waved one hand dismissively. "There's no reason to tell everyone everything, is there? I was saving my news for this retreat." She took in a deep breath. "I'm tired of safe and sweet. So, everyone, set aside your expectations of purple prose, warm embraces, and quickly beating hearts. This," she raised the typed pages, "is the good stuff."

"I'm interested." Logan's dark eyes were fixed intently on her.

"Yes, you have my full attention," Camille added.

Francie said nothing.

Dorn shook her pages as if stirring the words to life, then began reading. "The title is Blood on Shattered Glass. 'Blood was pouring from the wound in Alex's head. Staggering, she fell. She was trying to speak. She was staring at nothing. No one had seen her fall. Her corpse would be found later.'" She paused reading to give them a brilliant smile. "See what I mean? Good stuff. The rest is even better."

This is good? Liz asked herself. I must have missed something.

She shot a glance at Logan, who was frowning at Dorn. Camille's face registered confusion. Francie sat like the statue she'd portrayed earlier that day.

Dorn continued to read short choppy sentences, full of blood, wounds, and dismembered body parts. When she finished, Liz was queasy and troubled by the writing. In its own way, Dorn's chapter was as bad as Francie's. Maybe worse.

"My goodness," Camille said quietly, looking down at her hands as if reluctant to meet Dorn's eyes. "That is a departure for you. Completely."

"Agreed." Logan had not taken his gaze off her. "And you think that's better than your usual work?"

"I think it's brilliant. Don't you?"

He rubbed his chin. "Well, the plot has potential. A missing person always makes for an interesting tale. But it's full of the passive tense, and the way you've executed the scene gives me motion sickness."

"What's that supposed to mean?" She snatched up the papers as if afraid he'd take them from her.

"Vary your sentence structure. Smooth it out. Make it read like melted butter."

She glared. "Don't be ridiculous. Tense sentences build tension. That's one of the major rules of writing." She turned to Liz. "So what do you think? Brilliant, or simply good?"

Liz shifted uncomfortably and wished again that she had not agreed to sit in on the session. "I'm no writer."

"We know. Tell me what you think anyway."

Still Liz hesitated.

Dorn prodded. "You won't hurt my feelings. I've been at this a long time and I'm a professional."

Logan and Camille gave Liz a nod. Francie looked at Liz expectantly.

"Well, um, like Logan, I think the plot is intriguing. Suspenseful books and movies seem to use missing persons quite a bit."

"Are you saying the subject is overdone?"

"No, not at all. But I think you have too many short sentences too close together, so it seems—"

"Oh, what do you know? You said so yourself, you're not a writer. Camille, it's your turn to read." Dorn turned away from Liz.

A brief uncomfortable silence fell over them, then Camille said, "All right. This is the first chapter of the novel I'm working on. *The Second Week Alone*." She shot a nervous look around the group, then focused on the screen. "'The first time Susan saw the sunrise, she was eighty-seven years old.'"

Oh! Liz thought. If the opening sentence is any indication, this is going to be quite good.

Camille's chapter did not disappoint her. It was written almost musically, with rises and falls in construction and pace, each paragraph blending into the next, and a story that came to life on the page.

"Lovely!" she breathed when Camille looked up from the screen. Francie came out of her fog and clapped.

Dorn raised one eyebrow. "Very nice. An improvement over what you last shared in our group online."

Logan smiled in a way that took away the rigidity from his face and erased ten years from his appearance.

"That was great, young lady. As I've often said, you have talent. If you'll cut that middle part down, the story will flow better. Too much background too soon."

"Yes, weave it into the story instead of loading us down with all that information about her family." Dorn shuffled her papers and did not look at Camille as she spoke. Her tone was so dismissive that Liz sensed jealousy. "Your turn, Logan." She looked up and favored him with a warm smile. "Saving the best for last, of course."

His smile was a pleased one, perhaps even smug, as if he knew he was the best and being told so was his right.

"As you know, I've taken a hiatus from writing for the last couple of years, but I've come out of hibernation and started something new, The C.W. Black series. I've titled the first book Back From Yesterday. C.W. is a former FBI agent who chose to leave that career, go to medical school, and become a country doctor."

"Ooh!" Francie all but squealed.

"That's . . . different," Dorn said with a twitch of one eyebrow.

"Most authors would have probably written it with the career choices switched," Camille said.

"Which is exactly why I put a new spin on it. Give your reader something unexpected. Well executed, but fresh." He gave both Dorn and Francie heavy looks.

Dorn looked away, but Francie nodded eagerly. "I'll try to do mine better," she said.

He tossed her a quick smile. "Yes. I'll read now. 'Night crept, inch by inch, darkening every shape, fading every shadow, until at last blackness swallowed the world. The stranger stepped onto the narrow, winding path with complete assurance.'"

His listeners burst into applause and praise when he finished reading. The start to his new series promised the same intense writing and plenty of excitement, but the main character had more heart than his detective, Jack Todd.

"I hope that gets on the bookshelves soon," Liz said. "I want to read it."

"Thank you." For a moment, he looked humble and grateful.

"Me too!" Francie said. "I'll buy two of every book."

"That's kind of you to say." Logan gave her a quick nod.

"You've always been my mentor," Dorn said.

He frowned. "I have? Since when?"

She stared at him. "I mean, I've learned so much from what you've said in our online group, and I study your writing. So, in that way—"

"I see. But I'd hardly call that mentoring."

The women bombarded him with questions, and Liz lost the thread of conversation as she contemplated the group. Their dynamics puzzled her. She got the distinct impression that none of them really liked one another, although all three women openly admired Logan. That feeling might have stemmed from his having the successful career they all craved. His mature good looks no doubt underscored the admiration, and his brusque manner and underlying arrogance seemed to enhance rather than diminish that esteem.

He looked at his watch and said, "Critique time is over. We'll meet again this evening for a bit of socializing and a break from writing. Liz, I hope you'll join us then as well." Without waiting for a reply from anyone, he closed his laptop and got to his feet.

"Thank you," she said. "I'll provide some refreshments for your social hour."

"Yes, that would be nice. Ladies." He gave a little bow and left the room.

Dorn tipped her head to one side and watched as he left the room. When he was out of sight, she said, "He certainly sees himself as a ladies' man, doesn't he?"

"He does." Francie nodded.

"I can see why," Camille said. "He's incredibly handsome. Women probably chase him all the time."

"He's very handsome," Francie said.

Dorn made a face. "I don't care if he's incredibly handsome or looks like a toad. He's a good writer, and he knows the business. That's all that matters as far as I'm concerned."

"But you didn't take his critique with much grace," Camille said.

Dorn raised one eyebrow and held the younger woman's gaze for several seconds.

Sarah stepped just inside the doorway and asked, "Does anyone want anything else?"

"Not me." Dorn stuffed the manuscript folder into her briefcase. She got to her feet with only a bit of trouble. "Please show me to my room." She gripped her cane and walked toward the door. "I'll see the rest of you tonight."

"Dorn! Wait." Francie scrambled to her feet and hurried after the woman, clutching the laptop and her green bag. "You said you'd read my romance story, remember?"

Dorn shook her head and stumped out of the room, Francie followed right behind her like an eager puppy.

"Pathetic," Camille muttered as soon as they were gone. "I was hoping that woman would not show up after all, but here she is."

"Which one?" Liz asked.

"Francie, of course. When I found out she was planning to attend this retreat, I very nearly canceled my reservation. But I'm here to get as much help from Dorn and Logan as I can. Francie is the dark cloud to the silver lining." She rubbed her temple, then added, "Dorn is not as pleasant as I had hoped, but maybe she just needs some time to unwind. After all, she arrived and immediately got swept into the meeting."

"I'm sure you're right. I hope all of you enjoy your stay and find the retreat is both relaxing and rejuvenating."

"Thank you. I hope so too." Camille gave her a weak smile. "I've never wanted to be anything but a writer. It has been my focus for years now, and sometimes it seems as if I'll never reach that goal."

Liz laughed a little. "You are still very young. Give it time."

"I'm older than I look! I'm nearly thirty."

Liz smiled. "My goodness. I thought you were in your late teens or early twenties."

"Everyone does. And it's hard to be taken seriously when everyone thinks you're a kid. Logan and Dorn have both been so kind and so helpful to me online that I couldn't wait to meet them in person." She glanced toward the empty doorway, and a wrinkle appeared between her eyebrows. "But people aren't always the way you think they'll be, are they?"

Liz had a brief and bothersome image of Matt Sheridan, her erstwhile fiancé who had given every appearance of class and sophistication but had the character of a snake oil salesman, if not the snake itself. But then the image changed to the time Beans had made it clear that Matt was not welcome in his home. She almost smiled at the memory, then shoved the man out of her mind.

"Not always. But it's best not to think too much about the negative, is it?"

"Too right!" Camille smiled brightly. "I'm here in this lovely inn, getting to meet with my mentors face-to-face, and I am writing a book I absolutely love. Speaking of which, I need to get busy." She closed her laptop and stood. "Will you be at the social hour tonight?"

"I plan to be."

"Maybe you can keep Francie entertained while the rest of us enjoy the evening." She gave Liz another bright smile and left.

With these personalities, I think this is going to be less of a retreat and more of a minefield.

5

In the four-season room that evening, the guests seemed more relaxed and amiable. Liz served the German chocolate cake Sarah had made that afternoon and, for the time being, conversation centered on the mundane.

At one point Camille said to Liz, "I bet your life as an innkeeper is a perfect treasure trove of ideas for stories."

All of them regarded her with interest.

She chuckled, thinking of some of the adventures and misadventures that had happened since she took ownership of the inn. "Definitely. I've had a lot of interesting guests and plenty of mysterious incidents."

"Ooh!" Camille perched on the edge of her chair. "Do tell."

"Oh yes, do!" Francie practically twitched with excitement. She patted her green bag as if it were alive and needed comfort.

Liz began to share about some of the quirkier people who had come through her inn, but her audience kept asking about the mysterious incidents she'd mentioned. She wasn't certain sharing about the more shadowy occurrences was the wisest thing she could do, but they pressed her so vigorously that she relented.

"Well, there was the time Beans dug up some bones over by the lake," she began. "They were old bones, and they had a story." All four authors listened raptly as she related the tale, along with a few more incidents that had happened at the Olde Mansion Inn. While she talked, Logan pulled a small notebook from his pocket and jotted down a few sentences. Camille tapped in a few notes on her phone. Dorn and Francie merely gazed at her, almost without blinking.

"My goodness." Camille looked up from the screen. "Enough has happened here that you could write an entire mystery series!"

"I agree," Liz laughed.

"I believe you've given us all some ideas to ponder for future stories." Logan returned the notebook to his pocket with a satisfied grin.

"Yes," Dorn said languidly, tapping her cheek with one unpolished fingernail.

Sadie came in. She was dressed in red jeans, chukka boots, and a long-sleeved gray top. She carried an oversize red leather purse, and wore a red beret perched at an angle on her snowy hair. Lamplight bounced off the garnets in her earrings.

"Hi there!" she said brightly. "I hope I'm not intruding, but this is social hour. Right?"

Liz looked at her in surprise. The quilt shop had been closed for a couple of hours, and Sadie had not mentioned she planned to return that night.

Logan got to his feet. "No intrusion at all. Beautiful women are always welcome to our social hour." He indicated an empty chair near his. "Please have a seat."

Sadie's blush stunned Liz. Logan certainly had a way about him because it took a lot to embarrass her spirited friend.

"My goodness," Sadie murmured as she sat down. "I'm sitting next to a superstar."

He laughed. "Hardly that."

"Yes, you are. I love your books."

"Thank you for saying so. If you'll remind me before this retreat is over, I will give you a signed copy of one."

Sadie looked blissfully speechless.

Liz had never seen her friend this way, but she collected her wits and introduced Sadie to the group. "I'm sure you've noticed the Sew Welcome Shop here in the inn. Sadie is one of the owners. If you haven't visited the shop yet, please do. There are some lovely quilts on display."

"Are they for sale?" Logan asked Sadie.

"Oh, yes. And we sell fabric and notions of all kinds. And quilt patterns too." She glanced at the others. "Are any of you quilters?"

"I am!" Francie said. "I used to work in a quilt shop. Some of my quilts have won prizes."

Liz couldn't miss the skeptical look that passed between Dorn and Camille. Logan's eyes remained on Sadie.

"How wonderful! Be sure to come into our shop. You'll be so welcome at Sew Welcome." She laughed. "I'll have to remember that line the next time we put an ad in the newspaper."

Logan chuckled. "I like a woman with a sense of humor. And one who is not afraid of the color red."

Dorn rolled her eyes. "What about women who wear animal prints?" She was wearing a leopard-print top with black slacks.

He ignored her.

"There is a group of us who meet frequently and work on quilts together," Liz said, trying to steer the conversation in a safer direction. "We call ourselves the Material Girls."

"How cute." Dorn smiled, but her tone expressed complete boredom.

"Actually, I think quilt making and story writing might be a lot alike," Sadie said.

"Oh?" Logan's look of interest sharpened. Logan had not taken his eyes off Sadie since she sat down. She did make a compelling sight.

Sadie's blue eyes sparkled like sunlight on clear water. *Is she wearing eyeliner and mascara?* Liz leaned in for a closer look. *Yes, she is! And a little eyeshadow. And bronzer, for goodness' sake!*

Sadie must have wanted to make an impression, and from the expression on Logan's face she was succeeding. Liz bit her lip to keep from grinning. She reminded herself that the man was a charmer, and the last thing she wanted was for her friend to be hurt. But Sadie was no schoolgirl, and as eccentric as she was, she was also no fool. Still, Liz would keep a close eye on things and step in if necessary.

"Tell us how making a quilt is like writing a story." His voice was like warm honey.

"Yes, we want to know how making a quilt is like writing a story," Francie said, her gaze darting from person to person, as if seeking approval.

"Don't laugh at me," Sadie said, shooting a glance at Dorn, who gave her a slight smile.

"I wouldn't think of it," she replied.

"Never!" Francie declared.

"I love hearing new ideas," Camille added. "Please tell us."

"If you really are interested, and you seem to be . . . well, you know how one day you're out taking a ride, or going for a walk, or maybe even just washing the dishes, and an image comes into your mind all of a sudden? It might be the way the sunlight strikes a leaf and you see all the colors of the rainbow in that single green leaf. Or how raindrops make beautiful marks on dry pavement."

"Or how dried egg washes off when you scrub it in hot water?" Dorn added. She sent Logan a "can you believe this" look, but his attention remained on Sadie.

"I was thinking more about the bubbles—their fragility and iridescence," Sadie explained. "At any rate, something you see every day suddenly opens a door to all kinds of ideas you've never had before. And you think, 'How can I turn this thought, or this view, or this idea into a piece of art that others will appreciate?'"

"That's lovely," Liz said. "I never realized you thought that way,

Sadie, but it certainly explains your creativity with fabric." She glanced at the others. "You should see some of Sadie's patterns. They are so unique and beautiful."

"So how does this little arts and crafts thing equate to a story?" Dorn asked.

"Hush, Dorn. Let her talk." Logan's firm tone underscored the scowl he gave her, taking his eyes from Sadie for the first time since she'd entered the room.

Dorn frowned at him and clamped her lips together.

"Well, you start with that new idea, and you think how it would look with certain fabrics and stitching and shading. How everything would blend or contrast. Where problems might occur and how to solve them. Who it would appeal to so you can show it to them later." She shot a tentative glance around the room. "Isn't that pretty much what a writer does? Start with the idea, then consider all the parts and how they would go together to make a good story?"

"Exactly!" Logan beamed at her. "Have you ever written anything, Sadie?"

She blushed to the roots of her hair. "I've always wanted to write. I think I have a good idea for a book." She reached into her purse and pulled out some folded pages. "I have—"

"Everyone thinks they can write," Dorn muttered. "Everyone thinks they have a good book in them."

Sadie shifted in her chair and looked away, but not before Liz saw the humiliation that flickered across her face.

Camille scowled at Dorn. "Everyone *does* have a story in them."

"But not everyone should be writing it. Some stories are awful."

Sadie pulled herself together and cleared her throat. "I realize I'm not as talented as any of you. I never will be, I'm sure, but I did have this one little story I wrote a few years ago."

"Is that it?" Logan asked.

She nodded.

"Here, let me take it, and I'll read it tonight." He held out a hand.

Dorn, Camille, and Francie exchanged none-too-happy glances as Sadie passed the story to him. Did they think Sadie was intruding on their retreat? Then Francie looked at Logan, and burst out with, "I'll read it too!"

Sadie's smile showed her uncertainty. "I only have the one copy."

"One copy!" Dorn hooted. "A *real* writer never has only one copy."

Logan's expression turned dark as he glowered at Dorn.

Sadie threw a glance around the room as though seeking escape. "I've been thinking about having a party," she blurted.

Her announcement stopped any sharp words from forming, and the tense atmosphere mellowed.

"A party?" Liz said. "What kind of party?"

"Here, with you writers. And us. That is, the Material Girls and a few other friends. And Jackson, of course, if he's back from that municipal leadership conference in St. Louis. Since you're having a social hour every evening, I was thinking we could just expand it a little one night." Sadie shed her timidity, and the familiar take-charge Sadie came forth. "What do you think?"

"We're here to work, not party," Dorn said.

"To work!" Francie echoed.

Sadie sat back. "Oh. Well, it was just an idea."

"And a good one," Logan said. "It doesn't hurt to mingle with people. I'm trying to breathe some new life into my career, and a party is just what I need to blow off some of the dust."

"But when we organized this retreat—"

"A party!" Francie clapped, interrupting Dorn's words. "Let's have a murder mystery game. You know what I mean? A game where someone pretends to be murdered and the other guests have to figure out—"

Logan shook his head. "Something like that needs a lot of planning. Besides, there's no reason for party games. Just a little socializing. You *will* keep the number small, right?" He shot a look at Sadie and Liz.

"Of course. A small party is no problem." Remembering how her last murder mystery event went, Liz was not inclined to host another one anytime soon.

"And we Material Girls will provide everything." Sadie held up one hand when Liz started to respond. "This was my idea, so let it be my project. If you'll let us use the inn, I'm sure the other girls will pitch in, so no worries."

Logan grinned and jerked his head toward Sadie. "Is she always this bossy, Liz?"

Liz laughed. "No. Usually she's worse."

"I didn't bring party clothes," Dorn said.

"Neither did I." Francie tugged on one of her braids.

"Oh, no need to be fancy," Sadie assured them.

"I know! We could have a pajama party!" Francie looked at everyone else with the expectant bright eyes of child.

"Absolutely not," Logan growled at her.

"I'm not wearing my faded old jammies in front of anyone, let alone at a party," Camille said.

"Francie," Dorn said, "your online presence does not begin to compare with how you really are."

The woman cocked her head to one side, clearly confused as to whether this was a compliment or an insult. Liz wasn't sure either, but feared the conversation was about to take an ugly turn, with the clueless Francie as a target.

"Sadie, if you'll make the calls and invite our friends, I will be more than happy to host it here," Liz said.

Sadie beamed at her. "Wonderful! We'll have a great time."

"When are you thinking of having this party?" Camille asked. "This is Thursday, and we leave Sunday."

"How about tomorrow night?" She turned to Liz. "Will that work, Liz?"

"I'll make it work," she replied with a smile.

Sadie glanced at her watch. "I guess I should get started on those calls."

Logan stood and offered her his hand. "Allow me to walk you to your car."

She smiled and let him guide her to her feet. "Thank you." She passed a gaze over everyone. "It was nice to meet you. Thank you for letting me sit in. See you in the morning, Liz."

"Good night, Sadie," Liz said.

"Nighty night!" Francie called out cheerfully, hugging the green bag to her chest.

"Answer me this, Logan," Sadie said as they crossed the room. "What did one tomato say to another tomato during the tomato race?"

"I don't know. What?"

"Ketchup." She laughed loudly, and he joined in.

Francie giggled as the pair left the room, but Dorn sat stony and silent, watching the doorway as if expecting Logan to return immediately.

Camille gazed at Dorn. "Looks like we have another new member at our retreat."

6

Camille's observation was met with silence. Finally she turned to Liz. "Have you heard any more about the injured woman you found this morning?"

Dorn jerked, a deep frown slashing her forehead. "What injured woman?"

Surprised the others hadn't mentioned it to her already, Liz filled Dorn in on as few details as possible, then added, "Let's hope she recovers completely."

"Of course," Camille said. "What a terrible thing."

"Yes," Dorn murmured. "Disturbing."

"Surely someone is missing her and trying to find her by now," Camille said.

"Do you think so?" Dorn lifted one eyebrow. "What if she has no one?"

Camille put one hand to her chest. "Let's not even think that way."

Dorn twisted her lips to one side and her expression turned thoughtful. "There's a story in this. I'll bet Logan would agree." She looked expectantly toward the door again. After a few minutes, during which they made more idle chitchat and he still had not returned, she got up. "Since he's not back, I'm pretty sure our social hour is over. Besides, I'm tired. I'm going to my room."

"Me too!" Francie leaped to her feet. If Dorn even attempted to muffle her sigh, she failed miserably. She hurried from the room, but Francie kept up, dogging her footsteps.

Liz began to clear away the used cups and plates, but Camille's "psst!" caught her attention.

"Come here a sec," the girl whispered. "I want to talk to you."

Liz sat down in the chair nearest Camille and looked at her questioningly.

Camille twisted her hands in her lap. "This retreat is not what I thought it would be."

"Oh? What did you expect?"

"Not this." Her expression said Liz should know exactly what she meant.

"Is something at the inn not up to your expectations?" Liz hedged.

"No, your inn is beautiful and a wonderful place for a retreat. The views are inspirational. I love the Rose of Sharon Room, and I'm so glad you assigned it to me. I went up to the rooms on the third floor and looked around in them."

"You went up to the third floor?" She didn't know why she asked. Guests were free to poke around anywhere except Liz's private quarters and occupied rooms.

"Yes. I even sat on the floor of the Sunset Room and wrote for a while. But what I mean is—" she leaned forward and lowered her voice even more "—don't you find these people peculiar?"

While she agreed with Camille, she couldn't professionally say so aloud. "I've learned that everyone has his or her own peculiarities. It's what makes people interesting."

Camille made an impatient gesture. "I understand what you're saying, and I know you have to be careful about what you say about paying guests. But that's not what I mean."

"Okay. Go on, then."

"This is the first time any of us have met in person. As I told you this afternoon, I became acquainted with the other three when I joined the Master Writers Cooperative a few years ago. And it has been great. Logan started it as a way to offer help for beginning or struggling writers and as support for established authors."

"That was a very kind thing for him to do," Liz said.

"It has been wonderful. We share about writing, about books we've read, about conferences that we've attended, and editors or agents we've met. And we share bits and pieces of our work with one another for critique. Before I found the MWC, I attended a writers group in my town a few times, but it was more a 'tea and cookies' gathering than a real critique group. The MWC is so much better, even if it is online." She paused as if remembering something bittersweet, then took in a deep breath and blew it out. "Here's what has me bewildered. Online, Logan has been really encouraging to everyone. He's like a papa bear. If anyone has a difficulty with their writing, they go to him."

"That's great. You said he was your mentor."

"He has been. He's been so warm and helpful. But here, in person? He's . . . well, he has been a bit grouchy and impatient. I wanted to talk privately to him this afternoon, and he refused."

"I see. But you have to remember that this is only your first day, and after traveling, everyone is tired and not at their best. Maybe things will be different tomorrow after all of you have had a good night's sleep."

"I hope you're right. I can't help but wonder what he's going to say about your friend's story. Of course, he seems to like her, so . . ." Camille met her eyes, and something dark lurked in her gaze, as if she took perverse pleasure in thinking of someone else's discomfort. She dropped her gaze and shrugged.

Liz hoped Camille was wrong. Sadie had offered her story reticently, in a way that was unlike her usual bluster and confidence. Surely showing it to someone she admired was like offering up a piece of herself. Liz prayed Logan would treat Sadie's feelings with gentleness and respect.

"I'm not in the least surprised by Francie, of course," Camille continued. "She's as fruity in real life as she is online, if not more so. But Dorn is . . . well, I'm beyond surprised by her."

"Oh?"

"For one thing, her profile picture is way out of date. It must have been taken ages ago. All this time I thought she was about thirty-five, and that's not the case. That's not uncommon, though. People like to look good in their photos. And like Logan, she has been really warm and kind to everyone online. None of the nasty jibing she's been doing here. Dorn read my book a few weeks ago and promised to talk to her agent about representing me, and now she won't even discuss him or my book."

"Maybe that will change tomorrow. As I said, she's probably just tired, like everyone else. Consider that she had car trouble on her way here. And apparently she has a problem getting around easily. I imagine she's been in pain."

"Yeah, maybe." Camille gave her a half-hearted smile. "You're a nice person, Liz. I appreciate you letting me vent."

"We all need to vent sometimes."

"It's just that I *so* looked forward to this retreat and meeting my mentors. I even made myself a calendar and marked off the days." Camille angrily brushed away a tear. "I'm tempted to go home."

Liz understood her frustration. "Maybe your expectations were too high. Don't forget your mentors are people too."

"Yes, you're right. Maybe I wanted too much too soon."

"Before you make any drastic decisions, Camille, why don't you see how it goes tomorrow? I'm sure you will find that—" Liz's phone rang, breaking into the conversation. "Excuse me."

"Never mind. I'm going to bed," Camille said, getting up. "Thanks for talking to me, Liz. Good night."

"Good night. Try to get some sleep."

The phone chimed again. Liz glanced at the screen and answered. "Hello, Caitlyn."

"Hi, Liz. I thought you might like an update on the patient."

"Yes, I would." She sat up straight, preparing for the worst and hoping for the best. "Is she better?"

"I dropped by the hospital this evening and took a look at her chart. There's a note about possible brain damage."

"Oh no. That poor woman."

"Oh yes. She's still unconscious. I believe the doctor is going to do some further tests tomorrow. Have you heard anything more from the police?"

"I haven't, but I'll talk to someone tomorrow morning."

"Will you let me know what you find out so we can compare notes?"

"I sure will. Thanks, Caitlyn."

A bit later, when Liz took Beans on a short walk, Sadie was still outside with Logan. If the cold night air bothered them, neither one seemed to care. Liz wondered if a romance might be blossoming, or if their quiet voices were merely indicative of writer talk. She suspected a little of both.

Back inside, she gave Beans a biscuit, which he carried to his favorite rug. He rested his chin on it as though saving it for a midnight snack. Liz laughed and gave his broad head an affectionate rub.

"It's a dog's life, eh, Beans?"

He grunted in pleasure, wagged his stubby tail, and closed his eyes. She collected the used napkins, cups, and plates from the evening's socializing, then did her usual walk-through of the inn to make sure everything was tidy and ready for morning. She was halfway across the sitting room when something caught her attention. Or rather, the *lack* of something caught her attention. The small silver frame containing a photo of her sweet lazy bulldog was missing. She looked around to see if it was misplaced, but it wasn't. Then she noticed the much-used leather-bound Bible that had belonged to her mother was missing from the doily-covered end table where it usually rested.

Across the room, there was a gap on the shelf where a crystal candy dish had been. Her son, Steve, had given her the dish a few years ago, and it was precious to her, just like her mother's Bible, just like the framed photo of her dog.

Liz stood in the center of the room, her gaze probing every inch. Everything looked as it always did, except for the empty spaces where the trio of missing items belonged. She hadn't moved them, and in all the time Sarah had worked at the inn, she'd kept everything in its place. Her eyes moved to the closed door of Sew Welcome. People came and went every day to the shop. Perhaps someone had slipped into the sitting room unnoticed and swiped those three small items.

But why? They were worth very little, except as cherished keepsakes. Even the silver frame was just silver plate.

Maybe the person who'd pushed the unknown woman down the staircase had taken them. Liz squeezed her eyes shut, trying to recall seeing the objects earlier in the day, but she could not. She looked through every room again, this time more carefully. Nothing else seemed to be missing.

She went to bed, bewildered and more than a little uneasy.

She was awakened by a soft scratching on her door. A glance at the clock told her it was 1:32 a.m. Fearing one of the guests was ill, she threw on a robe and hurried to the door. When she opened it, Beans stood at the threshold, looking up at her through his soulful brown eyes.

"What on earth? I took you out before I came to bed."

He looked over his shoulder in the direction of the darkened kitchen. That's when she heard soft noises, as if someone was going through the cabinets. She belted her robe and, with Beans at her side, went into the kitchen and turned on a light.

Camille was crouched before the lower cabinets near the refrigerator with several pots and pans on the floor beside her.

"What's this?" Liz asked.

The young woman ignored her and looked inside a pot as if studying its contents.

"Camille?"

She looked up, her eyes unfocused.

"I thought I hid it in here," she said, "but it's all gone."

"Hid what?"

Rather than reply, Camille got to her feet and walked toward the doorway. She paused long enough to take a wooden spoon from a utensil holder near the stove, then left the room without a word.

"Camille?" Liz called softly, following her. But the young woman went upstairs, and a moment later Liz heard her door open and shut.

Beans had regarded the incident without a sound, as if he were recording everything for later consideration. He sat down and looked up at Liz. His wrinkled face was completely perplexed.

"Yeah, I don't understand it either," she said, "but I think we just witnessed a sleepwalker." She eyed the pots and pans, then crouched down to peer in the cabinet before replacing them.

What had Camille been looking for?

7

As soon as she'd showered the next morning, Liz called her close friend Jackson Cross, mayor of Pleasant Creek and owner of Cross Furniture Company.

"Good morning. I'm still at the breakfast table having my morning coffee." He chuckled. "If I'd known you were going to call me this early, I'd have at least combed my hair."

His voice summoned his image in her mind: a good-looking man in his mid-forties with hazel eyes and a smile that would warm the iciest heart. She visualized his brown hair mussed from sleep and smiled.

"Mine is wrapped in a towel. I wasn't even sure you'd be up yet after just getting back from that conference."

"I got home late last night and slept the sleep of the dead. Although I had a late night, and it's a cold, rainy, gray morning, I still woke up at six just like I always do."

"So how did the conference go? Did you have a good time?"

"I did, actually. And I met more small-town mayors than you could possibly imagine. Lots of talking, lots of information. Some good ideas I'd like to see developed in Pleasant Creek eventually. So how are things for you? The writers retreat going well?"

"Um . . . well, I'm not sure. They didn't get along very well yesterday, but they had just finished traveling. I'm hopeful today will be different."

"We've all heard about those artistic temperaments. It's been my experience that most creative people have their idiosyncrasies. Outside of the Material Girls, of course."

"You're right, but I'd still like to see them get along with one another so they can enjoy their time here. I'm trying to do what I can to make sure they have plenty of opportunities to have fun. Which is the main reason I called so early this morning."

"Oh?"

"I'm issuing you a last-minute invitation."

"An early last-minute invitation sounds intriguing. What's up?"

"There is going to be a small party here tonight, with the writers, the Material Girls and their spouses, and a few others. Sadie is organizing everything and she'll probably call you, but I wanted to make sure you had a personal invitation from me."

"I appreciate your thoughtfulness." His voice somehow grew warmer.

She smiled. "Does that mean you'll come?"

"I wouldn't miss it. What time should I show up?"

She opened her mouth to reply, then realized she had no idea when the party would start. "I'll find out."

"You let me know and I'll be there."

She hated to spoil the moment with her bad news, but it would come out sooner or later. "There's something else, Jackson."

"Oh? You want me to bring the chips and dip?"

She laughed a little, but sobered quickly. "No. It's about what happened here yesterday."

"That sounds ominous. What happened?"

Liz recapped the events for him. "And today I'm going to talk with the chief again. He didn't have much to say yesterday, but if he's holding back regarding something suspicious he found here, I need to know about it. I have a business to run and guests to consider."

"Law enforcement likes to play their cards close to their chest. You know that, Liz. But I understand your concern, and you certainly have a right to feel the way you do. How about if I talk to him for you?"

She appreciated the offer, but having Jackson save the day for her was not what she had in mind.

"You don't need to do that. Stan Houghton and I have had plenty of talks, you know."

He laughed. "But as mayor I might be able to get more out of him than you can, especially if circumstances are as suspicious as they seem."

She knew he was right, but she was hardly helpless when it came to digging up information. How would it look if she had Jackson asking questions for her?

"You have a town to run. I'll be going to the police station this morning."

"Are you sure you don't need me?"

Of course she needed him. She needed his friendship, his support, and his affection. But she refused to use his influence to make things easier on herself.

"It'll be fine. I'll let you know how it goes."

"Please do. I care about you, Liz."

The warm, fuzzy feeling around her heart grew. "Thank you, Jackson. That goes both ways."

"Call or text if you need me."

"I will. Talk to you later."

Sarah had the table set in the dining room and breakfast cooking when Liz went into the kitchen. It was warm and fragrant, chasing away the gloom of a cold, rainy morning. She glanced toward the utensil holder. The wooden spoon was still missing.

"Have you seen Camille this morning?" She kept her tone light and casual.

"I haven't seen anyone yet." If she wondered why Liz asked, Sarah kept it to herself.

Liz poured orange juice and placed a glass at each plate. She took a step back to study the table, making sure everything was neatly arranged.

"Good morning, Liz!"

She turned to see a smiling Francie. Dressed in dark capris, a white shirt, and red cardigan, Francie looked ready to take on the day.

"Good morning. I hope you slept well."

"I did. Your mattress feels just like my mattress back home. So comfy."

"That's wonderful. Are you hungry?"

"Yes!" She glanced behind her, and frowned. "I thought the others were coming. They were right behind me."

"They are. I hear them."

Francie sat down and looked expectantly at the doorway. She played with the red ribbons at the ends of her braids. The eager expression on her face unexpectedly reminded Liz of Beans when he waited for his supper.

Dorn and Camille came into the dining room, Dorn leaning heavily on her cane. They were in jeans and sweaters, and both looking rested and in a better frame of mind than they had the night before, although Dorn gave no friendly greeting. She sent Liz a frown as she sat down.

"Is your friend in her store?" she asked.

"Which friend?"

"The older woman from last night. She works in that little fabric store here in your inn, doesn't she?"

"Her name is Sadie, and she co-owns the quilting shop. If it's open already, she'll be there."

"Fabric shop, quilt shop, whatever." She waved one hand carelessly. "That's where Logan went. To see if your friend is in there."

"He likes her." Francie offered this piece of information as if revealing a delicious secret.

Dorn rolled her eyes. "We know that."

"He likes women in general. Or likes women to like him." Camille was on the other side of the room, eyeing Liz's collection of teacups. She picked one up, turned it over to read the maker's mark then set it back on its saucer with a loud clink that made Liz inwardly wince. Camille turned and came to the table. Her gaze seemed to challenge Dorn as she sat down. "Or didn't *you* know that?"

While the two women exchanged a glare, Liz eyed Camille, waiting for some word of last night's foray into the kitchen. If Camille did not bring it up, Liz would, but only when it was just the two of them.

"Did you both sleep all right?" she asked casually. "No disturbances?"

"I was fine," Dorn said.

"I slept well!" Francie said, grinning. "Like a baby. Like a log! I already told Liz."

Dorn gave her a strained smile. "Good."

"The Rose of Sharon Room is so lovely," Camille said with a smile. "How could anyone not get a good night's sleep in there?"

"Good. Well, I hope you enjoy your breakfast as much as your rooms."

Logan strolled into the room, looking cheerful and handsome in jeans, a white button-down shirt, and a tweed jacket. The subtle fragrance of an expensive men's cologne clung to him.

"Good morning, ladies," he said as he sat down. "You're a fine-looking sight first thing in the morning."

"We're hardly your first sight, are we?"

He aimed a puzzled gaze at Dorn. She gave him a chilly smile and sipped her orange juice. Liz could not help but wonder about the woman's apparent jealousy. Maybe there was some professional resentment between the two of them.

Sarah placed the food on the table and silently filled everyone's coffee cups. They turned their attention to fluffy scrambled eggs, crispy bacon, and flaky biscuits.

"Any news about that injured woman this morning?" Camille asked as she opened a biscuit and slathered it with Amish-made apple butter.

Liz had hoped no one would bring up the subject until she had information for them, but since all eyes were now focused on her, she shifted slightly in her chair and tried to think of the right thing to say.

"Didn't you ask Liz about her last night? I fail to understand why you are so curious," Dorn said. "It's morbid."

"I'm concerned, that's all. It isn't morbid to hope someone is getting better."

"Sorry, but I don't have anything new to report," Liz said.

"Do you think she's stable?" Dorn asked.

"I don't know. I hope to find out something today. Such a tumble might have caused brain damage, and if that happened, her recovery will take longer."

"Why, if that happened, she might *never* fully recover," Camille said.

"My goodness, how dreadful." Dorn picked up her juice and drained the glass.

"You still don't know who she is or how she ended up at the bottom of the staircase?" Camille studied Liz's face as if looking for signs of deception.

"No, I'm sorry to say. I'd like to know those details too."

"Well, we survived the night here at the Olde Mansion Inn, so let's stop prodding Liz for information she doesn't have or won't share." Logan met her gaze. She wondered if he was baiting her or trying to provoke her into telling more.

"It's very nice here," Camille added, as if trying to soften the mood. "And you have lovely things."

"Thank you." Liz's mind went straight to the spoon and the other missing items, but she needed to wait for the right time before bringing it up. Would there be a right time?

Dorn buttered a biscuit then put it on her plate, untasted, and shifted in her chair. She cleared her throat.

"I have something to say." She threw a side glance toward Camille. "It was brought to my attention this morning that I have been, well, not what you all may have expected. I will admit that the photo on my profile page was taken many years ago, and I really did not think anyone would care to know about my osteoarthritis or any other health concerns. I am not by nature a people person, and I deal better with them online than face-to-face. Deception was not my intention, and if any of you feel I have neglected you or bruised your feelings, I apologize. And since—"

"I forgive you!" Francie burst out, leaning forward eagerly.

"Yes, well, thank you." Dorn gave her a tight smile. "Since I have been coming across as rude and uncaring, I will now make a sincere effort to be congenial and jolly."

The wide smile she displayed hardly seemed genuine to Liz, and it probably failed to fool Logan and Camille.

Francie clasped her hands to her chest as if seeing a rainbow after a storm. "I think that's a lovely thing for you to say. Beautifully lovely."

"I accept your apology," Logan said.

"So do I. We should all remember a little courtesy goes a long way," Camille murmured.

Dorn's brittle expression clearly said she had not received the warm acceptance she'd hoped for, other than Francie's overly enthusiastic approval.

Silence fell, but the atmosphere in the room seemed stretched and fragile. The bright-eyed Francie was the only one of the four authors who seemed oblivious of any residual tension.

Liz tried to ease the mood. "I suppose today will be full of writing for all of you, won't it?"

"It will for me, I hope. Every day should be full of writing." Camille looked at Logan. "Don't you agree, Logan?"

He laid down his knife and fork, then placed his fingertips together above his plate as he favored each of them with a straight look. They stopped eating to give him their full attention.

"Perhaps 'full of writing' is too strong. Certainly, a writer should write every day if possible. Setting aside a time and a place to do so is essential to success. Don't make excuses or come up with reasons why you can't. Don't let anyone intrude on that time. However, you should not use your writing as a reason to lose touch with those around you or as an excuse to isolate yourself. Without interaction with others or new experiences to go through, you will run out of material."

Francie giggled, but said nothing.

"Do any of you keep a daily journal?" Liz asked.

Logan shook his head.

"I do!" Dorn said. "Faithfully."

"Sometimes I jot down things that happen to me," Camille said, "but not daily."

"Sometimes I do, and sometimes I don't," Francie said. "The fellas keep me so busy, I usually only have time to write about them and nothing else."

"The fellas?" Dorn lifted one eyebrow.

She nodded. "You know. The fellas I write about. Bobo and Tono. And the girls, of course. Riri and Sisi. And their friends and families."

Logan cleared his throat.

"If experiences are what we're after in our downtime, Logan, and they enrich our books, then you should write romance novels," Dorn said.

His spine straightened, and he frowned at her.

"A romance novel?" Liz turned to him with a smile. "Men don't usually write romance novels, do they?"

"Some do." He shifted his attention from Dorn to Liz. "All good books have a love story in them. Perhaps not the kind of romance we're familiar with, but love of some sort. Mother for her child, for instance, or a businessman driven by his love of making money. Even a child's love for her pet. Think about it. Every good book you've enjoyed has love at its core. It's the most basic human need."

Liz pondered his words for a bit. "I've never thought of it quite that way, but you're right."

"And let's not forget mystery," Dorn said. "There should always be some intrigue, something to be uncovered."

"And something to be attained," Camille added. "A character has to want something. Right?"

"Right!" Francie yelped.

Logan nodded. "Yes. A goal, something to strive for."

"Something the character will move heaven and earth to achieve," Dorn added.

"Even if it means breaking the law or causing pain to others?" Liz asked.

"Of course." Dorn said.

"A line has to be drawn somewhere, though." The frown was back on Logan's face. "If you have a character behaving badly, immorally, unethically, or even weakly, you will alienate the very person you need to support him. And that is who? Tell me, Francie."

She stared at him wide-eyed.

"The reader," Camille said.

"Yes!" Francie said, clapping. "The reader."

Logan nodded, smiling at Camille.

"And in romance novels, one needs to be faithful to his or her loved one. Or am I wrong, Logan?" Something about Dorn's expression told Liz there was more to the question than the words she asked.

"You're the romance author," he said calmly. "You tell us."

"Maybe I'm thinking about authors more than books."

Logan scowled at her. "What are you getting at?"

"You and that sewing shop woman. You're getting awfully chummy with her. Shouldn't you tell her about Madison?"

8

The air in the room turned cold, and it had nothing to do with the bitter weather outside.

"Madison and I are no longer together," Logan said through tight lips. "As if my private life is of concern to anyone here. And all of you can stop staring at me as if I'm diseased." He shoved back his chair and stalked from the room.

"Well, now," Dorn said after a few moments. "Overreacting much?" There was a smug little smile playing at the corners of her mouth.

So much for being congenial and jolly. She did that deliberately.

"I thought everyone knew about Logan and his women," Camille said.

"His *women*?" Liz asked.

"Don't you know? It's hardly a secret. He's been married several times, and he has so many girlfriends, I've lost count."

"Are you serious?"

"Our little Camille is a gossipmonger," Dorn said, almost affectionately. "She can dig up dirt faster than a backhoe."

Francie giggled.

"I am not a gossipmonger, Dorn, and you know it. But I am curious about things, and I like to satiate that curiosity. It gives me a lot of fodder for stories."

"If you use Logan Tracy for fodder without disguising him really well, you'll be handling a lawsuit."

"Oh, I hardly think—"

Dorn scooted back her chair. "You saw how upset he was by the mere mention of Madison? You go probing around in his private life and you'll find yourself in trouble."

"*You're* the one who mentioned Madison."

Dorn shrugged. "I just wanted to add a little interest to the morning. Can't let things go stale, can we? I'm off to my room now. I'll see you all this afternoon during our critique hour."

"Wait for me!" Francie got up, nearly tipping her chair over.

"Stay. Finish your breakfast."

"I'm finished." She trotted after Dorn, as she'd done before, like a faithful dog.

Camille stared at the empty doorway. "And here I thought she was going to make an effort at courtesy."

"Some people like to stir up drama. Maybe she can't help herself."

Camille glanced at Liz. "Maybe. But I refuse to let her ruin this retreat for me."

"So you've made up your mind to stay?"

"Yes. I talked with Logan this morning and shared how disappointed I was. He was really kind and understanding, and said I should stay. He also promised to talk to me privately about my manuscript."

"That's great."

She smiled. "And as you probably figured out, I talked with Dorn too. She said she had e-mailed her agent about my book and was simply waiting to hear back."

"I'm glad to hear it. It sounds like everything is moving forward for you."

Camille's smile grew bigger, and her eyes sparkled. "To be an author is all I've ever dreamed of. I'll do anything to be successful. Well, almost anything."

"I'm sure you'll succeed." Liz sensed the young woman wanted to say more, but was hesitant to do so. "Is something bothering you? Something I can help with?"

Camille took in a deep breath, scooted up on her chair, and shot a look toward the doorway as she leaned toward Liz.

"In spite of what Dorn said, I'm not a gossipmonger. I hope you believe me."

"I haven't had time to get to know you, Camille, but you seem to be a decent sort."

"Well, I may talk about people, but I'm not a gossip. Take my word for it. As I said earlier, I'm curious about a lot of things, human nature most especially. I refuse to squelch that because doing so would be like cutting off my lifeline to new ideas." She lowered her voice to a whisper. "But I do have something to say about Logan. I think he's terrific. He knows about life and writing, and he generously shares his wisdom. But he's a womanizer and, frankly, I'm concerned about your friend. You don't think she'll take his advances seriously, do you?"

"Didn't you say everyone knows about Logan and his many romantic ventures?"

Camille nodded. "You can find all kinds of stuff about him on the Internet, if you take the time to look for it."

"Then it's likely Sadie already knows."

"But she's older, and some older people don't like going on the Internet." Camille sipped her coffee and met Liz's eyes over the rim.

"That might be true for some, but not Sadie. She's a go-getter and doesn't let anything stop her, even technology. She's been a fan of Logan's books for a long time, and I imagine she's looked up information about him online. And I'm sure she finds his attention extremely flattering. Do you think there's a possibility of him being genuinely interested in her?"

"I've been in close contact with Logan for a couple of years now. In spite of his whole 'private life' speech just now, he has never made his interests a secret. So I was shocked to learn on a celebrity news site about his split with Madison. You see, he never mentioned one word about it to the MWC members, and I would have thought he'd at least say something about it."

"Maybe the breakup was more painful than usual."

She shrugged. "Maybe so. I've seen pictures of Madison. She's in her mid to late thirties, I'd say, and she's very beautiful. He should have been faithful to her."

"You think he wasn't?"

"I know he wasn't. He'd mention other women to our group sometimes, how he'd taken this one or that one out for dinner or dancing or whatever." She heaved a huge sigh and shook her head. "Maybe poor Madison got fed up and left him."

"He certainly seemed bothered when her name came up in conversation. Maybe he was in love with her."

Camille looked dubious. "Maybe so. Finally. But if that's the case, then he shouldn't have been dating other women when he and Madison were as good as married." She let out a deep, sorrowful breath and took another sip of coffee. "You know Dorn has a thing for him."

"I guessed as much." Dorn had an almost proprietorial air when it came to Logan.

"I never noticed it in our group," Camille said, "but of course, something like that could easily be hidden online. Maybe they private-messaged each other or something."

"He doesn't seem overly interested in her."

"I know. In fact, he seems annoyed by her." She stared down at her cup for a few moments. "Don't you wish people could be the way you thought they were?"

Liz gave her a kind smile. "That would certainly be simpler, wouldn't it? No second-guessing. No feeling caught off guard."

"Right." Camille drained the last of her coffee. "I should go to my room and work on the chapter I'm sharing in our critique session this afternoon." She started to get up, but slapped her forehead. "I nearly forgot! I woke up this morning with a wooden spoon on my pillow, and I forgot to bring it back down." She looked a little embarrassed. "I have sleepwalking episodes. I nearly always go into the kitchen and take something, and I must have done that last night."

"You don't remember?"

"I never do, but I've done it all my life. When I was little, I got a carving knife and took it back to bed with me. My mother nearly had a cow when she found it the next morning."

"I can imagine. "Liz wondered about the other missing items. It seemed likely Camille had taken them too, but why wouldn't she mention them?

"I'll bring the spoon back. Is it okay if I take a cup of coffee up to my room while I work?"

"Absolutely. Would you like me to fix you a carafe to take up with you?"

"That would be nice. And breakfast was really good. Thank you."

Liz looked at Logan's half-finished meal, and the food left on Dorn's and Francie's plates. "Thank you. I'll go get some pastries from next door for all of you, if you want something later. They'll be in the kitchen." Liz got to her feet. "I'll bring the carafe up when it's ready."

Camille stood. "You'll be coming to the critique meeting, right?"

Remembering the tension from the day before, she hesitated, but Camille's face took on a look of pleading.

"Please do. Your comments yesterday were well-thought-out and kind. Kindness is something we can all use."

"Then how can I decline? I'll be there."

After she took Camille's coffee to her, she peeked in at the quilt shop. Both Sadie and Mary Ann were involved with customers and two others were browsing. She decided to wait until she returned from her errand to talk to them. She got her purse and keys and drove to the police department where she sat in the waiting area for several minutes, wondering if she should have called and made an appointment. But she dismissed this idea, as Stan probably would have told her to stay home.

Minutes ticked by, and she tapped her feet. She was surprised when Jackson walked in. He glanced around the room, spotted her and strolled over.

"Well, hello," she said with a smile. "What are you doing here?"

"Good morning," he replied. "Just here as your sidekick."

She laughed. "My sidekick? Have you signed us up to play vaudeville somewhere?"

"Not quite. Actually, I—"

"Mr. Cross? Ms. Eckardt?" A young officer approached. "The chief's waiting for you."

They followed the fresh-faced young man to the chief's office. Stan shook their hands and invited them to sit. He and Jackson traded a few remarks about some municipal business and the conference Jackson had been to, and then he interlaced his fingers and parked both elbows on top of his desk. He shifted his sharp eyes back and forth between them.

"What can I do for you?"

Liz straightened her spine even more. "I'm still worried about the woman in the hospital. Do you know the extent of her injuries?"

"I know they are severe. She might have some brain damage." He frowned. "I'm sure you know this, Liz. Why are you here?"

I'm here because I want all *the details. I want to know who pushed her and why, and if you're trying to find the person who did it. I want to know if anyone in my inn is in danger.*

"I'm concerned. Since all my guests have arrived and she's obviously not one of them, I want to know what she was doing in my inn. And since there are no hazards that could have caused her to fall, I'd like to know how and why that happened, because I do *not* want it to happen again."

The chief simply looked at her without comment. She curled her hands in her lap and fought frustration. Jackson lightly touched her arm, a calming gesture. She took in and released a deep breath.

Stan shook his head. "At this point, we're waiting for her to wake up, and when she does, we'll find out who she is."

"But if she has a brain injury, she might not know who she is. She might not wake up for a long time. Or ever." Liz moved to the edge of her chair and leaned forward. She chose her words carefully. "Stan, you examined my inn thoroughly yesterday, and I got the distinct impression you thought she might have had a little help going down those stairs."

The chief said nothing.

"If someone else was in my home and injured this stranger, I have a right to know. And I need to know who and why. I need to know if my guests are in danger."

The chief looked steadily at both of them, then sat back.

"I'd like to help ease your mind, Liz. I really would. But there's really nothing much more to tell you. We do think she *might* have had help going down those stairs. And I trust you both to be discreet with that knowledge."

"Of course." She lifted one eyebrow. "Anything more?"

"Not at this time."

She and Jackson left the police station a few minutes later. He walked her to her car, then turned her to face him, a gentle smile on his lips. "I know this is frustrating for you."

"There are so many unknowns. I am trying to keep my guests happy and safe, but if there is any danger to any of them . . ."

"You are a strong woman, Liz, and you are up to this challenge. Do what you can, but trust our police department too. I will let you know the minute I hear anything."

She searched his eyes. "You promise?"

He raised his right hand. "I do solemnly promise."

She smiled. "Then that's good enough for me."

9

As soon as she got back from the police department, Liz went into Sew Welcome. Sadie was at one of the sewing machines, replacing a needle. She looked up as Liz approached, her face wreathed in a huge smile and her eyes sparkling. She was dressed in one of her nicer outfits, dark-maroon slacks and a cream-colored sweater. A bright pendant hanging from her neck gleamed in the overhead light.

A quick pang shot through Liz as she wondered if the extra sparkle was because of Logan Tracy.

"Did you have a late night last night?" she asked Sadie.

"Not too late." She bent over the machine and tightened the small screw that held the needle in place. "Logan is a fascinating man. Did you know he lived in Winchester for a time?" She straightened, leaned back in the chair, and gave a wistful sigh. "Fifteen years ago he was less than sixty miles from here, writing a book."

"I didn't know that."

"And just think, he's reading my little story today."

"Is he?"

She nodded eagerly. "And he invited me to the critique group this afternoon."

Remembering the stringent critique of Dorn's and Francie's stories the day before, a cold band tightened around Liz's middle. "Are the women reading it too?"

"Oh, I don't think so. I didn't ask them. And I don't think Logan will give it to them."

Her bright eyes and soft smile touched Liz's heart. "Sadie, you know having an author like Logan evaluate a story written by someone who is, well, inexperienced—"

Sadie tilted her head and gave her a curious look.

Liz tried to think of a nice way to say it. "His judgments might be a little hard to take. I mean, he's used to professional writers, so he might expect—"

Sadie waved one hand dismissively. "It's the same as if he asked me to look at a quilt he'd made. Since he's not a quilt maker, I wouldn't expect it to be on par with, say, your cousin Miriam's quilts. Or Mary Ann's. Or mine!" She laughed. "Get that worried look off your face, Liz. If he says it's the worst thing he's ever read, I'm ready for that. After all, how many people can say they've had their stories read by Logan Tracy?" Sadie deftly threaded the machine and checked the bobbin. She started to get up, but paused. "You have something else on your mind?"

"I do." She glanced toward a couple of women who had just entered the shop a minute earlier and were now browsing nearby. "Could I have a quick word with you in my quarters?"

All laughter left her friend's face. "Oh, dear. This sounds serious."

"Please?"

"Of course. Mary Ann, I'll be back soon."

Mary Ann raised both eyebrows from behind the counter, open curiosity in her gaze. "Okay."

Sadie quietly followed Liz back to her apartment.

"Have a seat." Liz indicated the settee in her small sitting room.

Sadie remained standing, her expression worried. "Are you all right?"

"It's nothing like that. But I do want to talk to you for a minute about a matter that causes me some concern."

"All right." Without taking her eyes off Liz, Sadie sat down. "What's this about?"

Liz perched in the chair next to her. "You're a good friend, and I hope you know that I care about you. The last thing a person wants is to see is a friend get hurt."

Sadie nodded, her expression bewildered and a little afraid.

Liz took a deep breath. "What do you know about Logan?"

"I know he's a good writer."

"I mean, what do you know about him as a person?"

"He lives in Florida and has no children. He likes comfort food. He's allergic to cats. What are you getting at?"

Liz looked down at her clasped hands and sought the right words. If she flatly stated what Camille had told her, Sadie's reaction would likely be something other than calm acceptance.

"I also know that he's been rather depressed for a while," Sadie continued, and Liz looked up in surprise.

"Oh?"

"He's tired of writing detective stories and wants to work on what he calls his 'big novel.'"

"So why doesn't he?"

Sadie shrugged. "Something happened a few months ago. It was serious enough to get him off track, and he missed the deadline for his book. He struggled to get it finished, and now he's having trouble writing the next one. He says he feels like he's at a crossroads and doesn't know which way to go. Isn't that terrible? To be that successful and talented, and feel lost?" She met Liz's eyes. "You know something else? He's a very lonely man."

"That doesn't make a lot of sense to me, Sadie. Yesterday he told us in the critique meeting about the new series he's writing, and he read part of the first book. It's very good, and he seemed quite excited about it."

"Oh?" Sadie frowned.

"He certainly didn't seem the least bit depressed or even ambivalent about it."

"My goodness." Sadie bit her bottom lip. "Maybe I misunderstood him."

"Maybe you did." *Or maybe he's just playing on your soft heart.*

"Anyway, I know for a fact that he has secrets," Sadie added. "When you ask someone something and they change the subject, it's a sure sign they're keeping something from you."

"That's true. And I'm glad you picked up on that, because—"

"Of course," Sadie said as if she hadn't heard Liz, "Madison walking out on him is probably what's at the root of all his unhappiness."

Liz gaped. "You know about Madison?"

"Oh!" Sadie pressed the fingers of one hand to her mouth and looked horrified. "Maybe I shouldn't have said anything. He said most people don't know."

"I won't mention it, but—"

"And then he clammed up. That's why I say he's got secrets. There's more to that relationship than he's telling." She nodded sagely. "Believe me. But I wasn't going to press him."

Liz thought about this for a bit, then cut to the chase. "Are you interested in him romantically?"

Her bright-blue eyes widened. "Logan and me? Of course not. What gave you such a notion?"

"The two of you seemed to get awfully moon-eyed."

"What a thing to say! Yes, he's a handsome fellow and yes, I'm a little starstruck, and yes, he's a sweet talker, but that doesn't mean we're romantically inclined. We share a mutual interest in creativity. In fact, he thinks he might like to try his hand at quilting." She folded her arms and looked smug.

Liz leaned back and stared at her. "Are you being one hundred percent honest with me?"

"Even if I were someone who lied, why would I lie about this? Why are you so concerned?"

"Because I don't want to see you get hurt."

"Hurt? *Me?* I've been around the block a few times, and I've known charmers even more charming than Logan. Believe me, I can take care of myself." She stared at Liz as though she had become transparent. Her expression changed as if she'd seen something disturbing. "Oh dear."

"Sadie? What is it?"

Sadie jumped to her feet and paced the length of Liz's small sitting room. She turned and said, "Do you think that woman in the hospital might be one of his old girlfriends, and somehow he sneaked in here while everyone was gone and shoved her down the stairs?"

The idea was so foreign to anything Liz had contemplated that she almost laughed. Then she sobered. It was as good a theory as any. But she just couldn't see Logan doing something like that. "Of course not. But you know him better than I do. Do you think it's possible?"

"Saying it out loud, I don't. It was just a foolish notion that popped into my head like foolish notions tend to do. Logan has been nothing but kind and gentle around me, and I don't think he's prone to any kind of violence. Just forget I said that. It was a stupid thing to say."

Liz didn't think she could forget, but she didn't believe it either. "Sadie, I just don't want you to be added to his trail of broken hearts without knowing what you're getting into."

Sadie smiled. "You are a mother hen sometimes, Liz. I admit it does bother me that he stretched the truth about being lonely and depressed if he isn't."

"Maybe he is. Maybe he hides it well. But he does seem excited about this new series."

Sadie was thoughtful for a few moments, then shrugged. "Everyone has their own peculiarities. Even me." She grinned and started to get up. "Was there anything else you wanted to ask or tell me?"

"Actually, yes. Did you notice anyone prowling or snooping yesterday?"

"We had our usual customers. Some of them take a long time to choose what they want, and sometimes it feels like they look at every bolt of fabric on the shelf. People like the Burgess sisters. But I wouldn't call their browsing snooping. Why do you ask?"

"Are the Burgess sisters the type who might pocket a few small items?"

"I hardly think so. They are tight with their money, yes. But stealing?" She shook her head. "On the other hand, you never know what people might do. Has someone taken something?"

Liz told her about the items from the sitting room.

"I haven't noticed anything suspicious, but we'll keep our eyes open for any pilfering."

"Thanks, Sadie."

After she was gone, Liz stayed in her quarters for a few minutes, running their conversation through her mind. Since she had come to Pleasant Creek and opened the inn, Sadie and Mary Ann had become close, trusted friends. If she had to be overly cautious and a little interfering from time to time, she would, because she cared for them. At least Sadie now knew that Logan could be deceptive if he chose to be, and she could be on her guard.

Was it possible Sadie's wild idea was right? Could the woman in the hospital be one of Logan's ex-girlfriends? Was that why he became so upset when Madison's name was mentioned?

That's too far-fetched to consider. It was just some silly idea Sadie's wild imagination conjured up.

Even so . . .

"Leave no stone unturned," she muttered as she left her apartment. She was halfway through the sitting room when she noticed the blue-and-white quilted lap throw that her cousin Miriam had made for her was missing from the end of the sofa where she usually kept it.

That's not a product of Sadie's imagination.

Liz checked in the four-season room for the quilt in case someone had carried it in there with them. Sarah was watering the large philodendron in the far corner. She didn't have the green thumb that Liz's other part-time employee, Kiera Williams, had. But now that Kiera was off at college, Sarah did a good job with the plants, and Liz told her so.

Sarah touched one of the variegated leaves with a fingertip. "It's a joy to care for *Gött's* creation."

Changing the subject, Liz asked, "Did you happen to launder the small quilt I keep in the sitting room?"

Sarah looked at her over her shoulder. "The one my mother-in-law made? No, but should I?"

"It's gone."

Sarah turned, a puzzled frown marring her smooth features. "Maybe one of the guests took it upstairs with them as extra covering." She looked out the window, and Liz followed her gaze. The gray sky hung leaden with a chilly rain. "Shall I build a fire for their meeting this afternoon?"

"Yes, please do. And keep your eyes open for the quilt, would you?"

"*Ja.*"

That afternoon, the cozy warmth of the bright fire chased away gloom and gave the room a homey, welcoming aura. Liz wanted to avoid the critique session, but Camille's plea earlier that morning had persuaded her to set aside that reluctance. She carried in cups and a carafe of hot coffee and placed them on a small table before the writers gathered. Standing perfectly still, she scrutinized every inch of the room. If anything else was missing, she didn't know what it was.

"Looking for something?" Camille's voice startled her.

Liz turned to see the young woman standing a few feet away, studying her curiously. "I'm just making sure everything is ready for your session."

"I'm ready." She lifted her laptop. "I've completed a key scene, and I'm eager to find out what the others think." She settled into an armchair.

"I think the scene you wrote yesterday was well done. Everyone seemed to like it."

Camille gave a genuine smile. "I worked hard on that. Thank you."

Liz poured her a cup of coffee. "By the way, do you know what Logan's most recent ex-girlfriend looks like?"

"Madison? I've seen photos of her. He has shared some pics of the two of them." She met Liz's eyes over the rim of the cup.

"What does she look like?"

"Petite, with long black hair. She's Asian, and quite beautiful. Why are you asking about her?"

Liz smiled. "Just curious." At least now she knew the tall blonde in the hospital was not Logan's Madison, and she could put that silly notion to rest.

When the other writers gathered, Liz was relieved to see they were a friendlier bunch than they had been. Logan seemed to have forgotten his earlier annoyance with Dorn, and everyone chatted casually while Liz filled their cups and each of them settled in a chair. Beans lumbered in and lay down, resting his head on Liz's foot. He twitched his eyebrows and met her gaze as if telling her he was there to ease her discomfort. She leaned down and stroked his soft ears.

"Good boy," she whispered.

Liz continued to feel uneasy until the actual critique got under way. The remarks were less caustic, and the suggestions given to Dorn and Camille after they read their chapters seemed helpful rather than discouraging, although Logan mentioned again how Dorn's writing was different from other work she'd shared. Dorn shrugged but made no comment, and he did not pursue it further.

All three women virtually gushed over Logan's scene. To Liz, it seemed too heavy on description when her interest had been on the conflict between two characters, but she felt awkward mentioning it. No doubt he had a reason to layer the words. Again, she thought of Sadie's comment about him being unhappy with his work. Maybe this scene reflected that discontent.

"I'm looking forward to reading the book," she said with a smile. Her brief comment seemed to satisfy him.

They turned to Francie, and as she had done the day before, she gave the impression of standing before her classmates in elementary school.

"I've written something new too." She beamed at Logan and Dorn. "Just like the two of you."

"Sounds intriguing," Logan said. "Read, please."

She cleared her throat. "'Once upon a time there was a very strong, tall, handsome, and smart detective named Todd Jackman. He solved many crimes. He was very smart. When a man was killed in his town, he went to the man's apartment and looked at the blood.'" She continued to read for twenty minutes, then looked up from her screen and beamed proudly.

Liz cringed for the woman—for the name of the detective so similar to Logan's mastermind sleuth, for her weak writing skills.

"What in the world was *that*?" Dorn asked after a moment's silence.

"The first chapter of my new book. I'm writing a mystery series."

"Don't tell me. The Detective Todd Jackman series?"

"Yes! How'd you guess, Dorn? You're so smart."

"For one thing, you've virtually ripped off the name of Logan's character and the name of his series," Camille said. "You can't do that."

"Why not?"

"Because it's stealing."

Her eyes got big. "You won't call the police and have them put me in jail, will you?"

"Oh good grief," Dorn muttered. "You're hopeless."

"Francie," Logan said, his voice far gentler than Liz had anticipated, "what you need to do is come up with something more original, a name and title that are all your own."

"Oh."

"And you have the same problem with this story as you had in what you read yesterday, and what you've written in all the stories you've given to me."

"You read them all?" She leaned forward eagerly. "Did you like them? Which one did you like the best?"

He held up one hand. "I looked through them. One of the problems is that you use the same words over and over. See if you can vary them."

"He's right," Camille said. "It is tedious."

She looked at them as if she didn't understand.

"Do you have a thesaurus?" Liz asked.

"I don't know."

"It's like a dictionary, and it will help you expand your vocabulary."

Dorn sighed loudly. "Get one. Use it."

"And maybe you shouldn't try to write books like mine," Logan said. "Stick with what you do best."

She stared at him, then suddenly laughed. "I know! I'll write about a mystery series about a detective elf. The RoRi Detective series."

Camille turned her giggle into a cough, then she coughed so hard she had to excuse herself.

Logan regarded Francie for a few seconds as if he could think of nothing to say, then he nodded. "Yes. Write that."

"Save yourself a world of embarrassment," Dorn said. "If you write it, don't ever publish it."

Francie's mouth formed a perfect *O*, but she said nothing as she gaped at Dorn.

There was silence until Camille returned, red-faced and wiping her eyes. She sat down without looking at anyone and kept fighting the amusement that returned several times to her face.

"Are you all right?" Liz said.

Camille nodded, not looking up. "Just a little frog in my throat."

"Yes, a lot of frogs in a lot of throats today." Dorn gave an exaggerated cough in her hand.

"So are there any questions or concerns we need to discuss before we break from this session?" Logan asked.

"I don't have a question, but I do have an observation." Camille raised her head at last. "I have to say I'm glad Patrice Barnhill did not show up to this retreat."

"Me too," Francie said.

"I thought for sure she'd be here," Logan mused.

"Poor thing," Dorn said softly. "She had planned to attend from the moment Logan organized it, but in the end she couldn't afford it. She e-mailed me this morning and wished us all well. Said she was going to spend the day writing along with us, just from her own home."

"If she'd come to this retreat and read that drivel to us, I'm not sure I could be kind," Camille said. "What I've seen of her writing is awful."

"Truly awful." Francie nodded enthusiastically as if grateful the negative focus had been taken off her own work.

"Did you see that goofy stuff she posted in our group a couple of weeks ago?" Camille asked. "I was so confused by it. What did it mean? Was it a war story? A sci-fi fantasy romance? A mystery?"

"She threw every element in a writer's cache into that thing," Logan said with a laugh.

"She did," Francie said. "Every single element. All of it."

Dorn scowled. "Well, I for one thought it was fine." The others turned to her, surprise on all three faces. "At least she's trying, which is more than can be said for a lot of people." She sniffed in irritation.

"There's trying, then there's doing. Even Francie is trying." Logan paused and looked uncomfortable, as if realizing what he'd just said.

Francie seemed to take no offense. "I'm trying, *and* I'm doing."

"Yes, well." Logan gave her a brief smile. "I've given Patrice a lot of advice but she becomes extremely defensive and ignores what I've told her. She'll never succeed if she refuses to listen. There will be no market for it, whether she finds a publisher or does it herself."

Dorn waved one had dismissively. "There are numerous ways to do marketing and publicity. If someone is clever enough, she can create publicity for herself in unexpected avenues. She can gain public sympathy, for instance. Or be controversial in her art and her approach to it. It's all in the plan the person chooses to implement."

Camille gave Dorn an exasperated look and shook her head. "It's all well and good to create buzz for yourself, but if all you are after is public notice and you have little regard for your book, what's the point?"

"Spoken like a true idealistic writer." Dorn rolled her eyes. "'Give me my garret, starve me, just let me have my art.' Meanwhile, in the real world, a lot of poor writers become best-selling authors because of publicity. At any rate, I happen to know Patrice personally. She's a warm, lovely lady with a lot of heart and a lot of talent."

"Yes, that's right!" Francie said.

"Oh, you know her and her work too, do you?" Camille's expression betrayed her cynicism.

Francie pulled on one of her braids. "Well, no. Not really."

"A minute ago you agreed with Logan and me that her work is truly awful, and now you're agreeing with Dorn that she's talented. Don't you have a mind of your own, Francie?"

"She doesn't have a mind, period," Dorn muttered in an undertone. Unfortunately, the room was quiet enough that her low words were easily heard by all of them.

"Oh, now, I see no reason to—" Liz began.

Francie clutched her green bag and laptop the way a child clutches an old blanket.

"I do so have a mind!" she said.

"You sway whichever way the wind blows, and you know it." Dorn glared at the other woman. "You agree with everyone, no matter what anyone says. If I were to look out the window right now and say the bright summer sun is shining in a cloudless sky, you'd agree even though it's dismal outside and raining hard." She leaned forward, jabbing her cane at Francie. "You are absolutely the most clueless person I've ever met in my life! You are unable to think for yourself."

Francie's mouth opened and shut like a fish. "You just . . . you just *hush*!" She leaped to her feet and ran from the room.

10

The others stared at Dorn.

"Well, that was one of the rudest things I've heard in a long time," Logan finally said.

"It was uncalled for," Camille added.

It seemed to Liz that most things Dorn said were uncalled for. She was one of the most malicious people Liz had ever met.

"Oh, give me a break. She has the brains of a grape, and you know it."

"Granted she doesn't seem very bright," Logan said, "and she annoys me to no small extent, but she's like a child."

Dorn glared at him. "As I recall, you battered her writing pretty hard yesterday, so don't pretend to be soft about her."

"Yesterday, I did not realize how fragile she is. Now I know. And so do you. She needs to be treated gently."

"And we also know that she is completely incapable of writing a good book, or even learning how to write a good book, so why waste our time? How she ever had enough sense to publish the ones she has out is a mystery to me. It takes a certain amount of savvy to self-publish."

"Maybe she had someone to help her," Liz said.

"I'm sure she did," Camille agreed. "But whether she can write well or not, she doesn't deserve what you just said to her."

"Oh, come on. She doesn't belong in our group. And you really shouldn't play so innocent and concerned, Camille. You've said some pretty ugly things about her."

The young woman's face reddened. "That might be true. I admit she gets on my nerves with all that giggling and agreeing and neediness, but I don't insult her to her face."

Dorn waved one hand as if dismissing Camille. She tapped her fingers against the cane and switched her gaze to Logan.

"Instead of being so high and mighty about the poor, talentless Francie, you should give Patrice a little more support. She reached out to you, believing you'd help her, and she expects you to keep your promise."

"Patrice e-mailed me some of her book."

She leaned forward expectantly. "And?"

He shifted impatiently in his chair. "We talked about this earlier, Dorn. I'm happy to help anyone who comes to me with the serious intention of learning about this business. But when my advice is resisted or ignored, there's not much I can do. If you're such a friend of hers, then *you* help her. Maybe she'll listen to what you have to say."

Dorn played with the tip of her cane, and her jaw was clenched so tightly Liz wondered that the woman didn't crack her own teeth. "So you're refusing to offer her any more help?"

"What's the point?"

"A couple of weeks ago, she posted in a group discussion that her work needs little to no editing," Camille said. "She pretty much said she's not changing it for anyone. I've not been writing as long as you or Logan have, but when a successful, experienced author offers advice, it makes sense to me that the newbie should at least consider it."

"That's right," Logan said. "I believe she doesn't want feedback or direction. She wants nothing but praise."

"What's wrong with that? Everyone needs a little applause now and then."

"I agree. But when someone gets only praise, how will that person ever learn how and what to improve? I sure got my fair share of criticism when I was a new writer. I'm sure you did too."

"Yes, I did. And I'm not convinced it helped." Dorn's jaw tightened and her eyes flashed. She stared hard at him. Logan held her gaze and seemed completely unfazed by her demeanor. She tightened her grip on the cane and pressed her lips into a thin, hard line.

"Liz," he said, turning to her, "you've been silent through most of our session today. Surely you have something you'd like to add to our conversation. How do you feel about the quality of writing that was offered this afternoon?" he asked.

She had hoped to avoid being put on the spot this way, but all three of them looked at her expectantly. She gathered her thoughts.

"As a reader, I am so impressed by all of you. And that includes Francie."

"Are you kidding?" Dorn squawked.

Liz offered a smile. "No, I'm not kidding. The amount of time and effort that goes into writing a story is admirable. To sit at a keyboard, or with a pen and paper, and put down words that become people and pictures, movements and events—that all takes enormous energy, doesn't it? As one of you said yesterday, a lot of people say they want to write, but they never do. All of you, including Francie, have done so. My hat is off to you."

"Well, you have a point," Dorn said grudgingly.

Logan chuckled. "Yes, you do. Your words ring far truer than the average person realizes. However, I believe you're holding something back. What is it?"

"Yes. Ask questions." Dorn's smile was bitter as if she wanted Liz to be cruel. "Put Logan on the spot. Tell us what you really think of Francie's bizarre little tale. Or ask Camille where she gets her ideas."

"What's that supposed to mean?" Camille asked.

"You know perfectly well what it means. Francie is not the only one who 'borrows' story ideas from others."

Camille scooted to the edge of her chair, her expression both astonished and thunderous. "Are you saying I steal ideas?"

Dorn smirked. "If the shoe fits . . ."

"Name one idea of mine that you think I've 'borrowed.'"

"The idea of a circus that never leaves town, for instance. That, my dear, was Patrice's idea, and you stole it."

Camille's mouth fell open. "I did no such thing! I wrote that story back when I was in high school."

Dorn scoffed and waved one hand dismissively. "Sure. Tell that one to Patrice's lawyer."

"*What?*" Camille's face grew bright red and she jumped up, both hands clenched. "I have my original draft, printed out, graded by my senior English teacher. So if Patrice thinks she can accuse me of stealing, she'd better have written hers more than ten years ago. That's when I wrote mine."

"Ladies! That will do." Logan's strong voice boomed over them.

Dorn stared back at her and said nothing.

A thought slipped into Liz's mind, something that might serve two purposes by halting the quarrel and uncovering a clue or two for her without raising any red flags.

"Come to think of it, I do have a question. Something I've wondered about from time to time."

The two women glowered at each other for another minute, then turned their attention to Liz.

"Let's say your main character is a decent, generous fellow with a lot of friends. But he's pretty sure one of his friends, whom he has trusted, may have done something illegal. He's unsure which friend, or friends, has committed this act, but he has his suspicions."

"Like what?" Dorn demanded. "Be specific."

"Let's say that the unidentified friend has stolen something valuable. The main character hates to think any of his friends could betray his trust, but signs point to it. How would your main character go about figuring out which one of his friends and acquaintances is the thief?"

"I haven't written anything like that," Camille said, still shooting daggers toward Dorn. "I guess the main character would go to the police."

"Not my kind of story." Dorn sneered and shook her head. "Ask Logan. He's the one who writes whodunits."

He gave her a dark look. "My novels go far beyond a simple whodunit, just as your novels go beyond a simple love story." Dorn's face reddened and her sneer faded. He turned to Liz. "My characters chase after bad guys all the time, but there are multilayered dynamics in a good suspense story. However, on a very basic level, the protagonist would look for clues. He'd start in the immediate area where the theft happened. He'd talk to the people who were nearby at the time whatever was stolen went missing. He'd ask if they saw something or someone out of the ordinary. He'd keep an open mind while he was at it, because he knows looks can be deceiving and everything is not always as it appears. A good writer would have plenty of misleading clues. Red herrings, they're called."

"He'd call the cops." Dorn said this in an offhand way, not even looking at the others. "Unless he is a cop. Which most of Logan's main characters are."

"But you said what if it was his friend, or friends, he suspected. Right, Liz?" Camille asked. "It seems to me that what the main character would do in this circumstance would depend on what kind of person he was, and the relationships he had with his friends. If he has a naturally suspicious nature, he might be a lot more aggressive toward those friends, accusing them outright. If he's kinder and more trusting, he'd be watchful, trying to pick up on clues that would tell him if the person was guilty or not. He wouldn't want to accuse a friend of theft unless he had solid proof."

"That makes sense," Liz said.

Camille looked at Logan. "What do you think?"

"You bring up a good point. Although in real life, we might not want to accuse our friends until we have proof, in fiction this kind of scenario would be ripe with conflict and emotion. The more upheaval your story provides, the more your readers will stay engaged in it. Keep them on the edge of their seats."

The writers looked at Liz, either waiting for her response or another question. Of the three, Dorn appeared to be shrinking, her energy and her wit diminishing moment by moment. Looking at her, noting her pale face, Liz wondered what caused the haunted look that now lurked in the woman's eyes. And was it possible that Dorn's abrasiveness was more a protective shell than an uncontrollable need to be insufferable?

Liz dragged her gaze away from Dorn. "I see."

Apparently Liz was more the trusting type, because she would not accuse any of them of taking her belongings unless she had proof. "Thanks for your answers. They were interesting."

Logan gave her a speculative look, as if he knew she had asked out of more than simple curiosity. They held each other's gaze for several seconds, then Logan broke the contact and stood.

"I'm going to take a little nap, then get some more writing done before the party Sadie is throwing tonight. And speaking of Sadie, have you read her story, Liz?"

She shook her head. "I didn't even know she had an interest in writing. It doesn't surprise me, though. Sadie is very creative, always full of ideas."

"Read her story sometime. Not bad. Not bad at all. In fact, it's better than some I could mention." He gave them all a little smile.

"See you later, girls."

"'Girls?' Get him." Dorn glared after him as he walked out of the room. "See ya later, laddie!" She gripped her cane, got to her feet and stood looking out the window for a minute. "I'd love to take a walk today."

"In the rain?" Liz said.

"Why not?"

"Well, it's pretty cold out there right now."

"I'll wear a hat and coat. Rain doesn't melt a tough old woman like me."

"That's for sure," Camille murmured.

Dorn gave her a half-smile, then excused herself and went to her room.

Camille closed her laptop. "Do you have a couple of cookies or something else sweet I can take to my room, Liz?"

"Sure. Come with me into the kitchen and get what you want."

After Camille left with a handful of gingersnaps, Liz went into Sew Welcome. Sadie was nowhere to be seen, but Mary Ann was ringing up a purchase. She gave Liz a strained smile and dipped her head to indicate someone in the workroom. Liz followed her gaze. Francie sat at one of the sewing machines. Its motor whirred at high velocity, creating a high-pitched hum in the room.

The customer left, and Mary Ann leaned across the counter. "She came in here a few minutes ago and asked if she could help make a quilt."

Liz glanced at Francie again, the small curved back, the elbows pointing out at ninety-degree angles from her body while she hunched awkwardly over the machine.

"She's wrecking it!" Mary Ann hissed. "She said she was an experienced quilter."

Liz grimaced. "And you believed her."

"I had no reason not to. I gave her the strips to join for that crazy quilt we're making for the church bazaar. She's already put over half of them together. No pinning, no careful stitching, just zip! through the feed and out the other side." She gave a soft little groan.

The sewing machine stopped, and Francie clipped the threads. She pulled the piece free of the machine, got up, and hurried to Mary Ann. "Here it is!"

Mary Ann held the piece out. A look of horror passed over her face as she eyed the uneven stitching, how the strips rippled and waved. She quickly changed her expression and gave Francie a forced smile that was as uneven as the seams in the quilt top.

"You like it?" Francie said. "I did it fast so you could put the rest of it together."

"Oh, um." Mary Ann cleared her throat. "Thank you."

"I want to do more. I'll just get those other strips." She headed toward a basket where individual fabric strips were ready to be joined.

"No! I mean, no thank you. I can finish this up."

"I want to help. My quilting group back home says my quilts are the best they've ever seen."

"Do they?"

Francie nodded enthusiastically, braids swinging. "So, I'll just get those others—"

"No, thank you."

"I want to do it!"

Mary Ann shot Liz a pleading look.

"Let's go have some tea, Francie," Liz said.

"Mary Ann needs my help right now, but as soon as I finish . . ." Her voice trailed and she looked from one to the other. "Wait a minute. You don't like what I did, do you?"

Mary Ann chewed her lower lip and looked miserable. "Francie,

I appreciate your enthusiasm. I wish more people were as eager to help as you are."

"I don't see what's wrong with it." Francie's voice and lips trembled.

Mary Ann and Liz exchanged a glance, then Mary Ann laid the piece out on the countertop, wrong side up, smoothing the hopeless mess as best she could. "This is a very good job. Thank you so much."

Francie stood as though frozen in place, shaking and white-faced. This had been the first time since her arrival that she had stood up for anything she wanted and been less than amenable to suggestions. Why had she suddenly chosen to stand against Mary Ann, who was kind and gracious, rather than Dorn, who'd been so brusque to her?

"Come on, Francie. Let's go have that cup of tea. I have some gingersnaps in the cookie jar." Liz held out a beckoning hand and took a step toward the door.

Francie shook her head. "No, thank you." She hurried from the room and ran up the stairs.

"Oh dear," Mary Ann said, looking stricken. "I guess I could have handled that better."

"I don't know how you could have. She was determined."

"Yes, she was that." Mary Ann hesitated, then added very quietly, "I believe there is something unbalanced about her."

"I feel sorry for her. She craves attention and practically begs to be noticed, but the others more or less ignore or dismiss her."

"Poor woman." They both looked at the empty doorway, as if she were standing there, alone and miserable. Mary Ann took in a deep breath and let it out. "What about the other writers?"

"What about them?"

"Are they anything like her?"

"No. They are unique personalities, just as everyone is, but I don't believe any of them is, as you say, unbalanced. And speaking of them, I suppose Sadie is busy preparing for the party tonight?"

"She is. We've had a slow day because of the rain, so I've been able to manage in here by myself. Logan Tracy made an appearance at lunchtime and took her next door for coffee and a pastry. She came back grinning from ear to ear."

"He told us a few minutes ago that he'd read her story and found it quite good."

"She said he told her it was a top-class story for someone who hadn't studied writing."

Liz smiled. "Then our Sadie is more talented than we realized."

Mary Ann laughed and rolled her eyes. "Don't tell her that. She's already chattering about writing a novel set in a quilt shop."

"You have an objection to that?"

"No. But I don't want to hear her crazy ideas for plots and characters either."

They laughed together.

"It's very generous of her to organize this party for the authors, especially on such short notice," Liz said. "I believe they are all looking forward to it."

Mary Ann smiled. "It's good of you to have it here."

"All I'm doing is providing space. Are you bringing pies?"

"I am! I made a couple of cherry pies last night, and when I get home I'm going to make a couple of pumpkin. Not exactly the season for them, but hey, who doesn't like pumpkin pie anytime?"

"Exactly!" Liz grinned.

"Naomi is bringing cookies and brownies. Opal is making a veggie platter with dip. Sadie is providing nuts and pretzels. Caitlyn has to work, so she won't be here. But we're going to have a good time. I invited a few others, but it will be small."

"There's nothing wrong with small."

"Oh, Liz!" she gasped. "I forgot to invite Jackson. How did I overlook him?"

Liz laughed. "I called him. We can't have a party with celebrities and not invite the mayor, can we?"

"Absolutely not." She started to leave but something in Mary Ann's face stopped her. "What is it?"

"I don't know. I just . . . After the incident with Francie, I'm a little worried."

"About her?"

"Yes. And about you. And the party. I don't know why, exactly. It's just a feeling that she might say or do something."

"I wouldn't worry about her making a scene, Mary Ann. She's not the type. I think she's just a little hurt and embarrassed that the quilt piece didn't measure up, and that's all."

"You're sure?"

"Pretty sure."

But after she left the shop, Mary Ann's worries lingered in Liz's thoughts, infecting her own peace of mind. The more she thought about it, the more uneasy she felt.

11

One of the first to arrive that evening was Naomi. Clad head to foot in rainwear, she brought in a stack of boxes filled with baked goods. The sugary fragrance wafted around her as she carried them into the kitchen.

"I brought a variety of goodies." She sat her haul on the counter and opened the top box. "When I read on Dorn's website that one of her favorite treats is chocolate pecan mini-pies, I found a recipe and made them for tonight." She slipped into the utility room just off the kitchen and removed her wet raincoat and galoshes.

Liz smiled and popped one of the bite-sized pastries into her mouth. "Ooh, these are scrumptious. Melts in the mouth. I'm sure she'll be delighted."

"I can't wait to meet her. I have her latest paperback in my purse, and I want her to sign it." The two of them began arranging the food on large plates.

"You and Sadie are such fans!" Liz said with a laugh. "Of course, Sadie's author of choice is Logan. The two of them are getting along like a house on fire."

She saw no need to mention the details of the conversation she'd had with Sadie. One thing she hoped was that the unpredictable Dorn would be as congenial to Naomi as Logan had been to Sadie. She'd hate to see that happy light in her friend's eyes dim because of a chilly reception or rude remark.

The doorbell rang. Sarah had declined an invitation to attend the party and had already gone home for the evening, so Liz hurried to answer it.

Jackson stood on the other side, his hair and clothes dampened with rain. He stomped his feet on the welcome mat to rid his shoes of any muck and held up a white shopping bag. "Dips and chips, as promised."

She laughed and stood back so he could enter. "Thank you, but you didn't need to bring anything."

Sadie bustled out of the sitting room and into the foyer. She wore navy-blue trousers with a soft white blouse. Her white hair was neatly styled with a slight curl, giving her a more youthful appearance.

"Hello, Mr. Mayor!" She grinned and held out one hand. "It's so good to see you, Jackson."

"Thank you. May I say you are looking exceptionally attractive this evening?"

"It's a party. I'm supposed to look gawgeous, dahling," Sadie drawled as she gave a little twirl.

"And you do."

She took his arm and said, "Give that bag to Liz, and you come with me." She batted her eyes like a coy debutante. He handed over his shopping bag and gave her an exaggerated bow, and then they walked toward the sitting room with great drama. Sadie burst out laughing before they reached the room, and Liz chuckled as she took the dips and chips into the kitchen.

Soon, Opal Ringenberg and her husband, George, arrived, along with several others. The sitting room was full of talk, laughter, and anticipation.

"Where are the writers?" Loretta Simmons asked. She was Pleasant Creek's head librarian. "I thought this party was for them."

"It is," Sadie said, "but I gave them a different time than you, because I want them to make an entrance."

"I see." Loretta twisted her mouth and wrinkled her nose. "I'm not much of a reader. I'm just here for the snacks."

Sadie paused, then seemed to realize the woman was joking. Sadie loved a good joke. The sillier it was, the harder she laughed.

"Knock, knock," she said, grinning.

"Oh, dear, here we go." Loretta blew out a huge sigh. "Who's there?"

"Rita."

"Rita who?"

"Rita a lot of good books lately?"

Loretta groaned and shook her head. "Sadie, you have an endless well of jokes, don't you?"

"I sure do! Which reminds me, what do Turkish librarians eat for lunch?"

Loretta tapped her index finger against her temple as though straining for the answer. "I don't know. What?"

"Shhh kebabs!"

"Good grief. I think that one calls for a cup of tea and one of Naomi's sugar cookies. Excuse me, Sadie."

Liz laughed as she watched the smiling Loretta walk toward the refreshment table. But her laughter died when local reporter Rob Carver strolled in, his red hair a beacon in the room. She reached out and grasped Sadie's forearm.

"Sadie! Why did you invite *him*?" She dipped her head toward the reporter.

Sadie followed her gaze. Her mouth flew open. "I most certainly did *not* invite him. Party crasher, that's what he is. I shall dispatch him forthwith." She slid a glance to Liz. "See? Being around all these writers has made me speak like a brainiac."

"That's hardly the word I'd use."

Sadie gave her a grin and started to move away. Liz stopped her. "No, wait. You know Rob and I are hardly the best of friends. If you throw him out of the party, he'll end up writing some kind of piece that will make the inn and the shop look bad."

"You think I should let him stay?"

"He's got his camera, and I can see his little recorder sticking out of his shirt pocket. He's here for a story about the writers. Let's offer him some refreshment, introduce him to them, and maybe he'll get his interviews and leave soon."

"You're sure you want to do that?"

"Yes."

"All right then. But if you change your mind, let me know."

"It's okay, Sadie. I know how to throw someone out of my house. Let's just hope he gets what he's after quickly. When will the authors show up, anyway?"

As if summoned, the four writers entered the sitting room and paused just inside the doorway.

"Here are our guests of honor!" Sadie sang out. Everyone smiled and clapped. Rob Carver hurried to the front of everyone, then darted here and there, taking numerous photos. Sadie ignored him.

"I'll introduce each of the authors, and then you can all meet them face-to-face. Standing nearest to me is the writer of a children's series called *The Little Ones*, Francie Sloan." Francie, in black slacks and white shirt, her salt-and-pepper braids freshly done and so tight they were stiff, clutched her green bag. She smiled awkwardly and stared at the group as if terrified of everyone.

"Next, we have Logan Tracy. He's the author of the Jack Todd mysteries and several other books as well. Logan is my favorite author of all time, as most of you know."

"We know, we know," Opal said. "You've gushed about him often enough over the years."

Everyone laughed, including Logan. He and Sadie exchanged a long look which made Liz question that "just friends" talk Sadie had given her earlier.

"The pretty young lady standing next to him is Camille Connor. She's a new writer, as yet unpublished, but I've been hearing some great things about her talent, so you better believe I'm looking forward to getting my hands on your first book, Camille."

The girl gave Sadie a big smile. "Thank you so much."

"And the last author is one I know you've heard of, especially if you like love stories." She looked at Naomi, who had not stopped staring at Dorn and grinning. "Naomi Mason there is her biggest fan. Dorn Alexander is author of over forty romance novels."

Dorn took a step away from the group, leaned heavily on her cane, and raised her right hand in greeting. When she smiled, which Liz rarely saw her do, she was quite attractive.

"Did any of you bring any books to sell?" Loretta asked.

"I have some in the trunk of my car," Logan said. "I always carry a few with me for times such as this."

"I have some too," Francie squeaked. She held the bag even tighter to her chest.

"I didn't realize we'd be having the opportunity to sell and sign books, so I didn't bring any," Dorn said with an apologetic smile.

"And I have none to offer." Camille winked. "Yet."

"You will soon, though," Logan told her. He looked at the partygoers and added, "Watch the shelves in the bookstore and libraries in a year or two. This young lady is going to be a sensation."

Camille blushed, but her green eyes sparkled, and her smile grew larger.

The party was lively and full of laughter as they got to know one another. Logan spun plenty of tales about his life and the adventures that had led him to turn to writing suspense novels. Rob moved through the room taking photos and listening to conversations. He pursued the authors and took notes. Finally, he left without a word to Liz, and she breathed easier.

Naomi talked with Dorn for a while, and later showed the author's signature to Liz.

"You have a treasured keepsake now," Liz said.

"I do!" She hugged the book to her chest the way Francie had hugged her green bag.

"And did she love your chocolate pecan mini-pies?"

A slight frown flickered across Naomi's face. "Funny thing, that. I told her that I'd made them especially for her, and she said she was allergic to nuts."

"Really?"

"I mentioned what I'd read on her website, and she said her site manager must have made an error because her throat swells shut if she eats nuts of any kind."

"Then that needs to be corrected as soon as possible. She didn't even let me know on the reservation form she filled out. There's a place to list allergies. What if I had served something with nuts or nut butter in it, and she ate it without knowing?" She shuddered. "It doesn't bear thinking about."

"I guess she overlooked it. But now you know."

"Yes, now I know."

They looked over the merry group. Nearly all the books Logan had brought with him had been sold, and Dorn and Logan had signed books the others had brought from home. Loretta bought one of Francie's for the children's department of the library.

"Look at Jackson. He's having a good time." Naomi gently elbowed Liz's ribs. "In fact . . ."

Liz followed her gaze. Jackson was on the sofa, Camille next to him, her head cocked saucily to one side, the light on her pretty face and shining auburn hair. She seemed intent on whatever he was saying. Francie sat nearby, gazing at Jackson like a lovestruck preteen.

"Maybe you should mosey on over there," Naomi said.

"Hmm. Maybe." But she stayed where she was.

"She's a lovely young woman." Naomi stared at Liz. "Don't you recognize flirting when you see it?"

Liz thought of Sadie and Logan, and how she'd misread that interaction according to Sadie herself. "Obviously not. Besides, there are others around who seem just as rapt as she is. George Ringenberg included."

"Well, if you're not going to break up that little tête-à-tête, I will."

Naomi started to move away, but Liz caught her arm. "No. Don't. It's not a tête-à-tête. Camille is very driven to succeed as a writer. She's not after Jackson, unless it's for information."

I hope.

Opal approached Liz and Naomi, holding a teacup and saucer.

"This is the most fun I've had in a long time," she said. "And Jackson is telling some of the most interesting tales about Pleasant Creek. Liz, you ought to go listen to them." She sipped her tea and met Liz's eyes over the teacup. Liz sensed immediately that Opal, in a subtler way, was offering her the same advice as Naomi.

"Come on," Opal said. "He's talking about the time someone thought Jaynes Lake had an alligator in it."

"An *alligator*? In Indiana?"

"Yes. You have to hear this."

She allowed Opal to draw her to the growing group around Jackson, who was saying, "I believe it was the most let down but relieved anyone had ever felt when they pulled that thing out of the water and saw it was nothing but a huge piece of tree bark that had caught some debris after a storm."

Laughter erupted, and Camille gave him a playful smack on the arm. Francie clapped her hands and brayed so loudly that everyone stared at her. Her laughter died, and her face flushed. She scooted back in her chair, cradling the green bag. Liz couldn't help but feel a twinge for the awkward Francie, who tried so hard to be liked.

She touched Francie's shoulder. "Would you like a cup of coffee or some tea?"

The woman stared sadly at her. "Me?"

"Yes. I'll be happy to bring you a cup."

"No, thank you."

"Maybe a cookie or a piece of Mary Ann's world-famous pumpkin pie?"

Francie shook her head. "No. I'm going to my room. Good night." She got up and hurried from the sitting room without another word. Liz followed with her eyes.

"How about that," Dorn said as she sidled up to Liz. "Francie embarrassed herself in front of everyone." Her lips were curled in a derisive smile.

"Yes, she did, and it's too bad. She's too socially awkward to understand how to deal with it."

Dorn waved one hand. "That has nothing to do with it. She's just plain weird."

Liz wanted to snap a harsh retort. Instead she excused herself and went to the beverage table. Dorn followed.

"I'll take a coffee, black, no sugar."

Liz poured it and handed it over, wishing the woman would follow Francie's example and go to bed before she offended someone. But Dorn seemed in no hurry to leave her side.

"Say, you have a handsome mayor in this town."

Liz coughed. "Yes. He is."

"Married?"

"No."

"Engaged?"

"No."

"Camille is extremely interested him, it seems. She's hardly spoken to anyone else. I can't help but wonder—"

Liz's cell phone rang. "Excuse me, Dorn. Hello?"

"She's awake," Caitlyn said.

Liz's heart leaped. "She is? Since when?"

"About half an hour ago."

"Has she said anything? Who is she?"

"She's not communicating yet, but we're hopeful."

"I'll be there as soon as I can."

"What about your party?"

Liz glanced around the room, noting everyone's smiles and relaxed postures. Jackson was now deep in conversation with George. Next to Liz, Dorn was sipping tea and openly listening to her side of the conversation. Liz was beginning to understand that writers had an insatiable curiosity that they never tried to hide.

"I'm pretty sure Sadie and the other Material Girls can take care of the party while I'm gone," she told Caitlyn.

"I don't know if you'll be able to see her."

"On my way right now. Thanks for letting me know." She ended the call and started to move away.

"Good news?" Dorn asked.

"Yes. It seems our mysterious injured stranger is finally awake."

Logan and Sadie were standing several feet away, but Sadie's sharp ears caught Liz's words. "She is? Oh, thank God!"

"I'm going to the hospital right now." Liz pocketed her phone. "Sadie, explain to the others and make my apologies, would you, please? I'll be back as soon as I can."

"Of course. You find out as much as possible and let us know."

"I will." She got her raincoat, purse, and keys, and left the inn quickly.

She was nearly to her car when she heard the sound of footsteps approaching fast. She turned, hoping to see Jackson wanting to accompany her. Instead, all she saw was a dark form a moment before something struck her hard, and then everything went black.

12

Liz woke up with pain pulsating in her head and a fiery ache in her shoulder. The ground beneath her was wet. Rain pattered against her face, soaking her hair.

What happened? Did I fall?

She pushed herself up into a sitting position and blinked a few times in an attempt to clear her vision. Slowly, she got to her feet, swaying a bit, then managed to stagger back to the inn and let herself in through the utility room door.

Mary Ann was in the kitchen making fresh coffee. She looked up and nearly dropped the pot.

"Liz, what on earth! Your head is bleeding. Oh my goodness." She helped Liz to the nearest chair, then wetted a dish towel at the tap. "Here, press this against your head. What happened?"

"I don't know. I must have tripped over something in the dark."

Mary Ann peered into her eyes, frowning. "What's the last thing you remember?"

Thinking hurt as much as the cut on her head, her sore shoulder, and the bright light in her eyes. "Putting on my raincoat to go to the hospital." She frowned. "I woke up out there in our parking area. This is scary. I can't remember if I got to the hospital. Maybe I was on my way back into the house from there."

"I doubt it. You left just a few minutes ago. But you're going there now. I'm taking you. Come on."

Liz obeyed, staggering a bit as Mary Ann led her to the car and helped her into the passenger seat. She had her phone out and was texting as she got behind the steering wheel. She sent the text, then they were on their way.

"I let Sadie know what was going on, then I sent Caitlyn a text to let her know we are on the way to the emergency room."

"Emergency room? No, no. I'm not going there, not for a little bump on the head. I want to see that woman who—"

"Right now, I don't care what you want," Mary Ann said as she pulled out onto the street. "You're going to the ER, and that's the end of the discussion. Sadie can manage here."

All the way to the hospital, Liz kept her eyes closed and tried to recall what had happened after she put on her coat. The memory was beyond her grasp. Maybe a doctor *should* examine her, but after that she had every intention of seeing the woman who had fallen down her staircase.

Caitlyn met them at the door with a wheelchair and helped Mary Ann get Liz into it. Mary Ann sat in the waiting room as Caitlyn wheeled Liz away.

"The doctor will be with you in a minute," she said as they entered a small examining room. "Let me take a look at this. I'll clean away some of the blood. Head wounds can be pretty messy, you know."

"I know." The image of the woman at the foot of the staircase popped into her mind, and so did the vision of blood on the walls, the newel post, and the stairs. She shuddered.

A few minutes later, a thin young woman with a brunette ponytail and huge black-framed glasses flung back the dividing curtain.

"This is Dr. Fullerton," Caitlyn said, then quickly filled the woman in on Liz's case.

The young doctor looked as if she were still in high school. But her approach to Liz was one of impressive professionalism.

"What happened?" She pushed the oversize glasses farther up the bridge of her nose and examined the damage.

"I fell."

"And what did you hit your head on?" She ran gentle exploratory fingers over the wound.

"I'm not quite sure." She raised her hand to touch the injured place and stopped, knowing it would hurt. "A rock? I don't know."

"This bruise has a definite oblong shape, so I don't think it was a rock. I need to disinfect the area. Now hold still. This might sting a little."

It stung more than a little, and the shot she received to deaden the area for stitches made her suck in a quick, hard breath.

When the wounds to her head and shoulder were dressed, Liz said, "I want to go upstairs to see that woman now that—"

"You are going nowhere but to X-ray," Dr. Fullerton said. "I want to make sure everything is as it should be inside your head. And depending on what we find, you'll either spend the night here or go straight home." She pinned a stern look at Liz. "There will be no going upstairs to anyone."

"Oh, but—"

"No buts, Liz," Caitlyn said firmly. "That patient you're so interested in will still be there tomorrow."

Her head throbbed, and the area on the side where she'd gotten stitches felt disconnected from her skull. Confusion hung around her like a thick fog. Getting the X-rays done and waiting while they were read by the doctor only added to her befuddlement. She lay in a softly lit room, staring up at the ceiling, trying to recall why she had fallen. Failing that, she tried to plot out a way to get upstairs to the injured woman. But it felt as though her mind would only allow her access to a certain amount of clarity before flipping the off switch.

The sound of voices and footsteps coming nearer distracted her from the task. She looked toward the doorway as Caitlyn entered, followed by Jackson. His thick brown hair was mussed and his tie was at half-mast. His normally confident and rugged expression was filled with anxiety.

"I found our mayor in the waiting room, pacing the floor like an expectant father in those old black-and-white comedies," Caitlyn said, clearly trying not to giggle.

Liz stretched out one hand to him. "Look at you, so worried."

He caught her hand and wrapped both of his around it. "Of course I'm worried. My girl's in the emergency room looking like she's been caught in a bad storm." He brushed her hair back from her face, his eyes taking in every aspect of her features, lingering on the bruises. "How are you feeling?"

"Woozy," she admitted. "Everything on and in my head hurts, including my hair and eyelashes. And I can't remember anything after leaving the party until I woke up outside."

"What are the extent of your injuries at this point?"

"You'll have to ask the doctor. Here she is."

"No serious injury that we can see," Dr. Fullerton said as she approached the bed. She looked at Jackson and recognition came over her face. "Hello, Mayor."

"Doctor."

They shook hands. "I believe my uncle went to high school with you. Andrew Fullerton?"

"I remember him. He was a senior when I was a freshman. Nice fellow."

Jackson returned his gaze to Liz and asked, "So she's all right?"

"She seems to be." She turned to Liz. "But I'd like to keep you overnight, so we can keep an eye on you."

And leave the inn untended? No way!

"I understand, but I have a house full of guests. I need to get back to them."

"Pardon me for saying so, Liz, but you are in no condition to be hosting or entertaining," Jackson said.

Caitlyn glanced at her watch. "Mary Ann called Sadie and updated her. I'm sure the authors are in their rooms by now, and the partygoers have all gone home. They're very capable people. They'll manage without you for a night, Liz."

"Listen to your friends, Ms. Eckardt," the doctor said sternly.

"Sorry, doctor, but I'm not staying." Liz sat up and swung her legs over the side of the bed. She fought a wave of vertigo.

"Lie back, please," Caitlyn said firmly. "My shift is over at midnight, and that's less than an hour from now. If you absolutely have to go home tonight, I'll come with you and stay the night."

"And I'll stay with her here until you get off work," Jackson said.

Caitlyn nodded and looked at the doctor. "All right?"

"It's not ideal, but if Ms. Eckardt is determined to go home, and you're willing to stay with her, then yes, it's all right."

"I think that's the best idea I've heard all day," Jackson said. He helped Liz settle back, and Caitlyn tucked the sheet around her.

"What about Mary Ann? Is she still in the waiting room?"

"I sent her home." Jackson's voice carried the authority of his office. "She was exhausted, and she's got a shop to run. And you might as well get it in your head that I'm staying right here until Caitlyn gets off work. That's final."

His words were firm, but a smile lurked in his eyes. A smile, and something more, something deeper, something Liz dared not put a name to yet.

"I'll stay," she said quietly.

"Good." He planted a kiss on the uninjured part of her head.

A few minutes after midnight, Caitlyn hurried in, her eyes big. "I went upstairs to check on that injured woman before we left," she kept her voice low. "Apparently there was an incident earlier."

A heavy frown drew Jackson's dark brows together.

Liz stared at her. "What do you mean? I didn't hear anything about an incident."

"You wouldn't. Internal reports of these types of events are kept as quiet as possible so patient recovery isn't compromised."

"What happened?" Jackson's grip on Liz's hand tightened protectively.

"Someone attacked her in her room."

"*What?*" they said in unison.

"And now there is a police officer at her door and no one is allowed to go in."

The news increased Liz's dizziness, and she dug her fingers into Jackson's hand. "But what happened? Who attacked her? Is she all right?"

"There was some kind of scuffle, and she was stabbed."

"Stabbed!" Liz gasped, her heart thudding.

"Not fatally, but badly enough that they've had to take her back to ICU. The person responsible got away before security arrived."

"That poor woman!" Liz said. "Someone really wants to hurt her, but why?"

"I wish I knew. I haven't even been able to find out her name. In fact, I don't know if she's talked to anyone. Everything about her and her condition is now basically on lockdown, and the police are investigating."

"Well, I need to find out what's going on." Once again, Liz sat up, preparing to get out of bed. "I'll go up there and talk to—"

"No you won't!" Caitlyn said. "If you go upstairs and insist on finding out who she is and what's going on, you could find yourself in a lot of hot water."

"But she was hurt in my place of business. I have a duty to my guests—"

"Caitlyn is right, Liz," Jackson said quietly. "There's a time to step up, and a time to step back. Right now, you need to step back. This seems to be a very dangerous situation, and no one wants you caught up in it."

"You have a duty to take care of yourself." Caitlyn's worried, doting expression and tone belonged on someone twenty years older and brought a smile to Liz's lips. "And as a nurse, and more importantly, *as your friend*, I have a duty to make sure you do so."

Jackson and Caitlyn had made valid points, and Liz knew it. She gave in to their pleas and was soon discharged from the hospital. In the parking lot, they got her comfortably into Caitlyn's car, and Jackson double-checked the seat belt as Caitlyn got behind the steering wheel. The glare from sodium lights in the parking lot pierced Liz's pupils like blades.

"You call me if you need anything, you hear? Either one of you." He glanced back and forth between them.

"Of course," Caitlyn said.

Liz gave a short nod which caused her head to feel like it might explode. She offered a thumbs-up instead, then leaned her head against the back of the seat and closed her eyes.

"Thank you, Jackson," she whispered.

He gave her a tender kiss. "I'll see you tomorrow." He looked across the car to Caitlyn. "Take care of her."

"You know I will."

"Yes. Thank you." One more brief touch of his hand to her face, then he shut the door and stepped back.

"Now that is a good boyfriend," Caitlyn said, and Liz agreed.

They had nearly reached the inn when a sudden thought burst into her mind, full blown. Her eyes flew open.

"Caitlyn! What if I didn't fall? What if the person who shoved the woman down the stairs knocked me out? And if that same person attacked the woman again tonight, whoever it is must still be out there, intending to cause more harm."

Caitlyn was silent for a few seconds. "Let's not think about that now. Let's focus on getting you comfortable so you can rest."

Somehow Liz doubted she would find any rest that night.

13

Liz showered under a warm, light spray, her hair and the wound on her head carefully covered with a shower cap. As the water flowed over her skin she reflected that if it were possible to sleep standing up, she would happily do so.

Once she was clean and dressed in her pajamas, Sadie and Caitlyn helped her into bed. After watching her as if they thought she might get up and walk out, Sadie turned off the light. Liz wanted to thank them for their care, but the moment she snuggled down into her comfortable nest, sleep took her until the comforting scent of hot tea wakened her.

She opened her eyes to a new day with sunshine at her window. Steam rose in a fragrant cloud from a cup on her bedside table, and she caught sight of a blue skirt hem slipping out of the door.

"Sarah?"

The young woman stopped and came back into the room, her blue eyes watchful and concerned. "*Guta Morgan*. I hope I didn't wake you. How are you feeling?"

Liz stirred. The pounding inside her head was still there, but less intense. The vision in her swollen right eye was a little blurry. The scrape on her shoulder had ceased its burning torment, but joint and muscles ached as she hoisted herself into a sitting position. Sarah handed her the cup.

"Better. Thank you."

Sarah never took her eyes off Liz's face. It was almost as if she expected Liz to do or say something extraordinary. "I'll fix some *Stümorga* and bring it to you."

"No, no. I'm not reduced to having breakfast in bed. Have the authors come downstairs yet?"

"Not yet, but I've heard them stirring."

"I'll get dressed and help you fix breakfast."

"Drink your *Tee* first, for strength. Do not hurry. I will start the Stümorga."

Liz had caught sight of herself in the mirror after her shower last night. She had looked exactly the way she had felt—bruised and in pain. That morning, as she peered at her reflection in the bathroom mirror, she appeared only marginally better. The right side of her face was puffy and purple, one eye half-closed. She cringed from the merest touch of fingertips on the sensitive area. At least the scrapes on her sore shoulder were minor, obviously caused when she hit the ground, and the pain had diminished significantly.

She winced as she applied her makeup with gentle fingers. Her appearance was off-putting, but since there was no help for it, she resolved to move through the day as if nothing had happened. The morning's grooming and dressing took longer than usual, but when she emerged from her quarters she was clean, her makeup smooth, and her blonde hair styled as neatly as ever. The loose black pants and long-sleeved pink blouse fit her frame smartly. In spite of her bruises, she still looked like the friendly and efficient innkeeper she was. At least that's what she hoped.

"Liz, how are you?" Sadie rushed to her the moment Liz stepped into the quilt shop. "Oh, my." She reached out as if she might touch the bruise, but stopped and withdrew her hand.

"I'm fine. I just wanted to say good morning, and thank you for the party. You did a great job getting everything together at the last minute."

"I enjoyed doing it," Sadie said absently, still staring at her. "Should you even be out of bed?"

"Yes, I'm fine," Liz repeated. "A little bruised and sore, but that's to be expected after a fall as hard as the one I took."

"I'm glad Caitlyn stayed over last night," Mary Ann said, joining them. "I sent her home when I got here this morning, but she's planning on coming back later." She, too, fixed her gaze on Liz's injured face.

"She's terrific. If she hadn't volunteered to stay here, I believe she might have hog-tied me to the hospital bed to keep me there overnight."

"She's a good girl." Sadie met Liz's eyes, then lowered her voice. "She told me what they suspect about that woman."

"She told you about that? When?"

"While you were in the shower. I know it's confidential, but she thought I should know, seeing how I was helping to take care of you. And so I could keep my eyes open for . . . well, anything or anyone that might be . . . you know, suspicious."

Mary Ann frowned. "What are you two talking about? Told you what?"

"The police think that woman falling down the staircase was no accident. And I'm pretty sure that Liz's injuries were no accident either."

Mary Ann's eyes widened for a moment. "You mean they think someone pushed her?"

"Right, but you can't go repeating that," Liz said, glancing around to make sure they were alone.

"Of course not."

Sadie nodded. "We're going to be keeping our eyes open, though. You can depend on that."

"Do you think Caitlyn told Jackson?"

"Maybe. Caitlyn is a good employee, but she's also a loyal friend. She might have felt he should know."

"I won't mention it unless he does," Liz said. "Speaking of which, I should call him and let him know I survived the night. Excuse me, ladies."

She left Sew Welcome and settled behind the reception desk in the foyer to make the call.

She had just hung up when the front door opened, and a middle-aged couple rushed inside. Their faces were drawn, and their demeanor screamed urgency. They looked around as if seeking something vital.

"May I help you?"

"Yes!" the woman said. "We're the Scotts, Marvin and Agnes, and we're here to take her home."

"Who? The only guests I have right now are four authors—"

"Francie Sloan is here, isn't she?"

"Yes, she's still upstairs. Is she your sister or some other relation?"

The woman nodded, then for the first time seemed to really see Liz. She stared at her bruised face and pressed her fingers to her mouth. "Oh, no! I am so sorry! We had no idea—I am *so* sorry. When did she do that?"

Liz looked back and forth between them, astonished. "You think Francie . . . ?" She touched the bandage.

"She's done it before," the man said. "More than once."

Mary Ann and Sadie hurried out of the shop and into the foyer, clearly alarmed by the woman's distressed tone.

Liz gaped at the man and woman, unable to speak for a moment. "Francie . . . ?"

"We'll pay your medical bills, of course," the man offered. "Has she done anything else? Did you call the police?"

"Are you saying Francie gets violent?" Mary Ann said.

"My wife's sister is not well."

"She never has been," his wife added in a whisper.

Was it possible Francie had caused Liz's injuries? Was it possible she had pushed the unknown woman down the staircase? Liz's thoughts tumbled like stones in a rockslide.

She found her voice. "Francie has acted a little odd at times, but I had no idea she could hurt anyone."

"If she's known to be dangerous, why didn't someone tell Liz before now?" Sadie demanded.

"Because we had no idea where she was! And she's not dangerous. Not usually."

"Calm down, Agnes," the man said. "She's here, and we'll take her home." He looked at Liz. "Francie lives in a group home where she is taken care of and monitored closely. They make sure she takes her meds on time and is kept calm. But she ran away a couple days ago and no one knew where she'd gone."

"Then how did you trace her to here?"

"After they called and told us she was missing, we went straight to Hanniford House and searched through her things for any clue as to where she might have gone. Marvin found the notebooks she'd hidden under her mattress." Agnes looked at her husband, who nodded. "She had written in there about her plans to attend this retreat. Apparently she'd been putting aside money to pay for this trip from the allowance we give her."

"But it must not have been enough, because it seems she stole cash from some of the other residents," Marvin added.

A dangerous thief staying in her inn, and she'd fooled them all with her childlike demeanor. It was enough to make Liz shudder.

"How in the world did she get here all the way from Kansas?" Agnes asked. "Don't you do any kind of background check?"

"I'm in the business of accommodating strangers who come to our town for a visit. No, I don't do background checks."

"Did she call you, or just show up, or what?"

"She filled out a reservation online like my other guests."

"May I see that?"

"Of course."

Liz opened the registration files on her computer and pulled up Francie's record. She turned the screen so Marvin and Agnes could view the information.

They looked at it, and Agnes made a strangled sound and pointed at the screen. "She made all that up. Look there. My birth date as the driver's license number and our old phone number for the plate. She doesn't have a car. She doesn't even drive!"

Liz mentally shook her head. She didn't normally verify the plate numbers of the cars parked in her driveway. She wondered how Francie had gotten to the inn. It would have taken some doing to get to Indiana from Kansas, but where there was a will, Liz supposed there was a way.

"Your sister wouldn't know the truth if it bit off the end of her nose." Marvin's words drew a scowl from his wife. Liz suspected this was not the first time they'd had words with each other about Francie.

"My sister is good-hearted and will say or agree to anything if she thinks it will help build a bond with others. Where is she?" Agnes looked around as if she expected Francie to be standing in the middle of the room.

"Probably in her room. I'll tell her you're here." Liz started to move away when she heard Logan's voice upstairs talking to someone. "Maybe I won't have to do that. I believe the writers are coming down for breakfast."

She heard Logan's rumbling chuckle and Camille's light laugh, then a second later Francie's shrill giggle. "Me too!" she cried out as she trailed the other two down the stairs. "I love waffles with lots and lots of butter and syrup!"

"Even after that party last night, I'm ready for a productive day of writing," Logan was saying to Camille as they descended.

"But breakfast first. Liz is wonderful about making sure we start our days off right."

"I smell the waffles. I hope Liz is all right this morn—" Camille saw her and broke off with a gasp. "Oh, my goodness, Liz! Look at your poor face. How are you feeling?"

"Not as awful as I look." She forced a smile. "I'm sure Sarah has breakfast ready for you."

Behind Camille and Logan, Francie halted on the stairs, green bag on one arm, eyes wide as she silently stared at her sister.

"What on earth did you hit when you fell?" Camille asked.

"Other than the ground, I'm not sure exactly. I'm sorry to have missed so much of the party."

"But are you okay?" Logan's features were serious, his eyes studying her face. "That's the important thing."

"Yes, I'm all right. A little sore, a little bruised, but—"

"*You!*" Francie shouted, pointing at her sister and husband. "What are you doing here?"

"We're here to take you home, Francie," Agnes said gently.

"No!"

"Listen here," Marvin growled. "We drove all this way, and you are going back to Kansas with us right now!"

"Actually, the police need to talk to her first," Liz said.

"*Police?*" Francie screamed. She clutched the green bag as if her very life depended on its contents. "No, no, no!"

"Calm down, for pity's sake," Agnes said. She turned to Liz. "We don't need to involve law enforcement with this situation, Ms. Eckardt. We've already told you we'll cover your medical bills. Just forward them on to us. Marvin, give her our address. And rest assured that Francie will be returned to Hanniford House when we get back to Kansas. So there is nothing more to be done, and certainly no need to file charges against her."

"I didn't do anything!" Francie shrieked. Her eyes were wide and wild. "I've been taking my medicine. I've been keeping myself clean and my hair brushed and braided. I've been writing my stories. I've been caring for the Little Ones."

She patted the bag as if to soothe it. In that moment Liz finally understood why Francie had kept the bag with her at all times and why she was so protective of it. Francie believed the green bag housed her invisible friends.

"You must be the one who shoved that woman down that flight of stairs," Sadie said, pointing.

Liz stared wordlessly at Sadie. Why had she blurted that accusation when only a few minutes ago they had talked of how important it was to keep the information under their hats?

"Oh my goodness!" Camille gasped. "She is? No way!"

Francie's mouth flew open, and Agnes gawked at Sadie. "She did? When was this?"

"I did no such thing!" Francie ran down the stairs and practically knocked her sister over as she clung to her. "Aggie, you have to believe me. Marv, don't let them take me to jail. I can't go to jail. You know I can't go to jail!"

Agnes pushed the clutching hand away and stepped back. "Stop that right now."

Agnes's voice was firm, but not unkind. The order froze Francie in place once more. "Go upstairs and get your things. And give me the Little Ones," Agnes continued. "I'll take care of them."

Francie shoved the green bag at her sister and fled up the stairs, her braids bouncing as she ran.

"You can see she's little more than a child," Agnes said as soon as Francie was out of sight. "She is neither malicious nor intentionally violent. But when she doesn't take her meds, she has very poor impulse control. Even so, I hardly think she'd shove someone down the stairs."

"Sadie was making an unfounded accusation based on fear and rumor," Liz said, giving her friend a warning look, "but when you saw the bruises on my face, *you* immediately assumed your sister did it, didn't you?"

Agnes winced. "Well, yes. But I assumed it was because she wasn't taking her meds, and someone had said or done something to upset her."

"How can you be so sure she's been taking her medication?" Sadie asked. Mary Ann gripped Sadie's forearm, but Sadie paid her no mind. "You haven't been here to watch her."

"Because when Francie is off her meds, she does . . . other things."

Sadie grunted. "I'm sorry I flew off the handle, but Liz was attacked and I guess I got protective of her. How is Francie different without her medication?"

"For one thing, instead of braiding her hair, she ties it in knots," Marvin said. "And she purposely puts her clothes on inside out or backward. She'll speak in syllables and words only she understands. She'll drink vast amounts of milk. We haven't figured that one out."

Agnes turned to Liz. "Has she done any of those things?"

"No," Liz said. "She's been well-groomed and articulate. I haven't noticed any odd or excessive eating habits. She does seem hungry for approval—"

"She's always wanted to make friends. It gets her into all kinds of scrapes if she's left on her own. That's why she's at Hanniford House, where she can be properly cared for."

"But she's dangerous." Sadie glared back at Agnes.

"No, she isn't. Not if she's taking her meds. She is far too interested in playing with her Little Ones and writing her stories about them to even think of causing problems." She turned to Liz. "I don't know what happened to you, but since my sister seems as well-adjusted as ever, it's quite obvious she did not attack you. And if someone took a tumble down your staircase, she either fell on her own or you need to look elsewhere for the person who shoved her. And now I'm going to go help Francie." She pushed past everyone and ran up the stairs.

"I'm sorry this has happened," Marvin said. "Francie is childlike, as you no doubt know by now, but she is also clever. She's obviously been planning for this so-called retreat a long time." He frowned and studied them as if looking for defects. "What I can't understand is how and why she knew about this place. Do you advertise it as a mecca for needy writers or something?"

"We are an online writers group," Logan said, "and Francie has been a part of the group for a couple of years."

Marvin looked both skeptical and outraged. "You mean she makes friends with people she doesn't even know online? Who else has she been meeting?"

"She's a member of our group, and I am glad to have her." Logan kept his voice quiet and even, but Liz sensed the underlying tension.

Marvin narrowed his eyes. "I'll speak to the Hanniford House administrators about this. She can't be allowed to pick up strangers on the Internet. It's not safe. Why is someone like her on the computer anyway? She is perfectly happy to play with her dolls and imaginary friends. That's what they should make sure she does, rather than become involved with who knows what kind of people."

"You're right," Logan said. "Francie is much too trusting, and the Internet presents a lot of danger, especially to vulnerable people like her. You should be sure to follow through on talking with the people in charge of the facility where she stays. However, we would like her to remain part of our writers' group."

"I agree," Camille said firmly. "If Francie enjoys being part of our group, I am glad to have her."

Marvin looked surprised. He cleared his throat. "I'll talk it over with Agnes and the staff at Hanniford House. I guess there's no harm in her writing her stories with all of you, but we will have to set some limits, for her own safety."

Agnes and Francie rushed downstairs, luggage banging each step as Agnes pulled it behind her.

"But I want Logan to read my detective story," Francie wailed as she trailed her sister. "And Dorn still hasn't read my romance yet."

"Come on, Francie," Agnes said. "It's time to go. Marvin, take Francie's bag and help her to the car, will you?"

"Yes, dear. I will." He took Francie's arm in one hand and steered her toward the front door. She neither protested nor balked, though she did send a look over her shoulder that was filled with considerable sorrow and resignation.

"Goodbye, Liz. Goodbye, Logan. Goodbye, Camille. Goodbye, Dorn." She continued her farewells, chanting them like a mantra as he herded her outside. In less than a minute, Francie, her belongings, and her family were in the car and gone. The inn seemed oddly quiet.

"My goodness," Liz said faintly.

"Aren't you going to call the police?" Sadie said. "That woman is bonkers."

"Yes, she is, but mental illness is not a crime."

"She left the party before you did, Liz, so she wasn't with the rest of us. I think she walloped you, which is assault. And that *is* a crime."

"So is shoving someone down a staircase," Camille added. "Not that I'm convinced she did it, but we have to consider the possibility, I guess."

"I can't prove Francie knocked me out or pushed someone down a staircase. Francie's family is taking care of the situation, and she will soon be where she's safe and taken care of. I see no reason to add to their problems by going to the police with an unproven theory."

Sadie turned to Logan. "What would Detective Jack Todd do in a situation like this?"

He gave her a smile. "This is real life, not a story. I think Liz is wise in her decision."

"Sadie is our mother hen," Mary Ann explained, giving Sadie an affectionate poke, "trying to keep us all safe in case the sky is falling."

Logan's smile deepened. "Not a bad trait to have."

Did Sadie have a valid concern? Liz ran a rapid review of the situation in her mind, and on the surface, it seemed likely that Francie had caused the havoc and injury. She was decidedly odd. She watched others with an intensity that could make most people uneasy. She had displayed over-the-top reactions while at the same time being oblivious to the needs of others. She had left the party early. But she had displayed none of the symptoms that indicated she'd stopped taking her medication, according to her sister.

If Francie had not pushed the woman down the staircase, who had? For that matter, was Liz's injury a result of being hit rather than falling? If so, who had hit her? She had no answer for that, but the attack on the woman in the hospital underscored her feeling that someone was still out there. And that person had no qualms about hurting someone else.

Liz wished Sadie had remembered her promise to keep silent about the woman in the hospital. Her biggest hope now was that the authors would turn their focus to their retreat—and that she hadn't just let a dangerous person leave town.

Liz shook her head. She'd tell the chief about it, and let him decide what to do. "Let's not let the waffles get cold," Liz said. "Shall we go have breakfast?"

"Sounds wonderful," Camille said.

Mary Ann and Sadie returned to the quilt shop as Liz led the others into the dining room.

"Dorn isn't coming down this morning?" she asked as they settled at the table.

"Maybe she's sleeping in," Logan said. "She's not a young woman, and might not be used to staying up as late as we did last night."

"I think she went up to her room before we did, though," Camille said. "She's probably working. She mentioned yesterday that she's nearly finished with her manuscript and hopes she can get it done in the next day or two."

"I see," Liz said. "Well, I'll make sure she has something to eat in her room."

Silence fell over the group for a minute or so as they ate, then Camille spoke up.

"I know she was a nuisance, but it seems weird that Francie is gone."

Logan drizzled more syrup over his waffle and shook his head. "It's . . . quieter. And is it bad that I feel somewhat relieved? I know you'll only agree with me if you genuinely agree."

Camille laughed. "I've never known someone as agreeable as Francie."

"But I hope she gets the help she needs and is safe."

"I'm sure all of us hope for that," Liz said.

"Of course," Camille murmured.

Logan speared a bite of his waffle and glanced at Liz. "Do you think she's the one who hurt you and that other woman?"

Liz forced a smile and a bright tone to her voice. "It was dark and rainy outside last night, and I think it's far more likely that I stumbled and cracked my head when I fell." Even as she said the words, a shadowy something trickled into her conscious. The memory of a sound, a swift movement—but it faded abruptly.

"It doesn't hurt to be cautious and watchful, Liz."

They ate in silence for a while, then Camille turned to Logan. "I need to talk to you about one of my characters trying to take over the scene."

"Fire away."

While Camille and Logan chatted, the shadowy memory crept around in Liz's brain like a cat stalking prey. It pawed softly at her, then retreated, then returned, trying to get her attention. When she tried to focus on it, it disappeared again, only to return with that same feline stealth.

"What do you think, Liz?" Camille's voice drew her back.

She shook her head to clear it. "I'm sorry. I drifted away for a moment."

"Since it isn't raining today, Logan and I were thinking of taking a walk around the lake before we start writing. Is it likely to be very muddy?"

She followed their gazes out the window to the sparkling water of Jaynes Lake. "The path is pretty hard-packed. If you stay on it, I believe you'll be all right."

After breakfast, the two donned jackets and set out across the backyard. Liz cleared the dishes from the table.

"You may go ahead and clean the Somewhere in Time Room and change the bed linens, Sarah," she said as she prepared a tray for Dorn. "Francie will not be returning."

"All right." True to her nature, she asked no questions or made no observations, though surely she was curious. How much had she seen or overheard that morning? Liz was confident Sarah had continued with her work in the kitchen, neither spying nor eavesdropping. Not that Liz would have blamed her. But that wasn't Sarah's way, or the way of most of the Amish Liz knew.

She carried the tray upstairs and knocked on Dorn's door. "It's Liz. I have some fruit and muffins and a carafe of coffee for you, Dorn." When the woman did not respond, she added, "I'll leave it next to your door, and when you're finished you can put the empty tray out here."

An hour later Liz was sweeping the front porch when Sarah approached.

"The guest's tray hasn't been touched, and she did not answer my knock."

Liz frowned. "That's troubling, because she didn't answer me either. I wonder if she's all right."

She put away the broom, and they both hurried up the steps to the Heirloom Room. The tray of food was exactly where she had placed it earlier.

Liz knocked. "Dorn?" She waited a few seconds and knocked louder. "Dorn, are you all right?"

The door downstairs opened, and Logan's and Camille's voices wafted up as they came inside. A few moments later they appeared in the upstairs corridor, smiling and rosy-cheeked from their walk.

Logan's smile slipped away. "Everything okay?"

"I'm not sure," Liz said. "Have either of your seen or spoken with Dorn this morning?"

"Not me," Logan said.

"I haven't seen her since before the party ended last night." Camille glanced at the door. "Is something wrong?"

"I don't know, but she's not answering us."

"Maybe you weren't loud enough." Logan stepped up to the door and thumped on it. "Dorn!" His voice was like thunder, and Liz winced. When Dorn did not answer, he turned the knob and the door opened.

"Not locked!" Camille said.

Logan strode into the room and the others followed. "No one is in here." He pointed to the bed, still smooth and pretty, completely untouched. "And it looks like no one *has* been in here."

14

"Has something happened to Dorn?" Camille asked. Her eyes were wide.

"I wish I knew." Liz looked in the bathroom, noted the fresh towels still unused and folded from yesterday. The sink and shower were both dry and sparkling. "The last time I saw her was at the party. I poured her some coffee, and we chatted a bit."

"She was having a good time," Logan said. "At one point, I noticed several of the ladies had her cornered and were asking all kinds of questions about writing romance novels."

Liz looked at Camille. "At breakfast, didn't you say she went upstairs before you did last night?"

"That's right. Or at least I think she did. I was having so much fun talking with everyone that I wasn't paying much attention to her."

She peeked inside the wardrobe. Dorn's slacks and blouses still hung on the clothes rod. A hatbox was on the upper shelf. She turned to the dresser. An array of cosmetics littered the top: a dusty powder box not quite shut, a lipstick on its side, an open eye shadow container, and several brushes. A medication bottle caught Liz's eyes. It was smudged with a ragged label, as if it had been carried with Dorn a long time and to many places. Liz picked it up and noticed her name had been worn off. She could make out the name of the medication though.

"This is for diabetes. Surely she wouldn't go somewhere without medication. That could be quite dangerous."

"I didn't know she has diabetes," Logan said. "She never mentioned it."

"She never mentioned a lot of things," Camille replied. "One thing I've learned while I've been here is that Dorn harbors plenty of secrets. I suppose she wants to build and maintain the mystique of a romance author."

For Liz, the woman's absence was far more worrisome than a simple case of "author's mystique."

"Maybe this is not a circumstance of her keeping a mysterious persona. In light of what we just learned about Francie, don't you find Dorn's absence even more disturbing?"

"Are you suggesting Francie had something to do with this situation?" Logan asked.

"I'm simply pointing out that one author has been taken away in less than peaceful circumstances, and another hasn't been seen since last night."

Not to mention it seems more and more likely someone knocked me out, and very probable that the same someone pushed a visitor down the staircase.

She suppressed a shudder. Logan and Camille stared at her as if assessing whether Liz herself had had a hand in the nefarious doings. She pulled her phone from her pocket and dialed Dorn's number. It rang several times but she did not answer it, and the message Liz received was short and simple: "This person does not have a voice mail account."

"Nothing. Maybe she's taking a long walk," Liz suggested as she pocketed her phone.

"Since last night?" Camille said.

"Maybe she left early this morning, before anyone got up, and made her own bed. She may have gone farther than intended, and because of her arthritis, she's making her way back more slowly than we would. Did you see any signs that she might have been along the lake?"

Logan shook his head. "There weren't any fresh footprints on that wet path. I tend to notice things like that."

"I'm afraid that wherever she went, she didn't go willingly," Camille said.

"She's older, she's not in the best of health . . ." Logan stroked his chin. "It wouldn't take much to overpower her. A small person could do it."

"She said some mean things to Francie," Camille said. "We all heard her."

"True enough. And who knows what she said to her when we weren't around."

"Francie interacts online with other writers in your Master Writers Cooperative, doesn't she?"

"Oh, does she!" Camille said.

Logan nodded, a half smile on his face. "Right there agreeing with everything."

"You heard her brother-in-law, though," Camille said. "I hope he doesn't arrange it so she's not allowed access to the Internet again."

"That would be a shame," Liz said. "It seems a better arrangement would be closer monitoring for at-risk people like Francie."

"Maybe that's what they'll do." Camille's voice lacked conviction. "And she does seem to enjoy her writing. It would be a shame to take that away from her."

"Has Dorn been as unkind to Francie in your group as she is in person?"

"Not at all. Dorn offers all of us a lot of encouragement and good information about the business. She shares links to sites for writers that she thinks might help us." Camille flashed her warm smile. "She even got in touch with me and volunteered to read my manuscript. After she read it, she said she loved it and asked if she could pass it on to her agent. Maybe she did the same for Francie, but it really seems unlikely, doesn't it? I mean, Francie isn't . . . that is, her writing is . . . and Dorn isn't as . . ." She gestured helplessly.

"Never mind, my dear. We know what you mean." Logan gave her shoulder a fatherly pat. "But an author has to maintain a friendly online persona if he or she wants readers to connect with them. It's not at all unusual for someone to be completely different in real life. I know many authors like that—some famous ones, too."

"One of the last things Francie said as she left was that Dorn hadn't read her romance book yet," Liz said.

"If this retreat has taught me one thing, it's that Francie is more imaginative than truthful," Logan said. "I doubt Dorn offered to read anything she wrote."

Liz agreed he had a valid point. On the other hand, Dorn had said and done some peculiar things too. It was possible that she had told Francie she'd read her manuscript simply to torment a woman who aggravated her so much. She recalled a conversation from the day before.

"Do you remember yesterday when Dorn mentioned something about a writer creating publicity for herself?"

Logan's eyes widened. "Now that you mention it, I do."

"You aren't suggesting that Dorn has staged her own kidnapping, are you?" Camille asked. "I mean, really. Would she do something like that, as old and disabled as she is? It would be a brilliant move, though. Remember how Agatha Christie disappeared for eleven days back in 1926? To this day, no one really knows what happened to her."

"I'm not suggesting anything," Liz clarified. "I'm just mentioning the idea of it. Let's not get too caught up in suspicion and fear until we know more."

"I couldn't agree more." But a frown continued to crease Logan's brow, and his dark eyes probed every inch of the room. "I've always thought of Dorn as a top-notch professional, so I'll be surprised and disappointed if she's simply taken off without a word. But let's not forget that Francie had affixed herself to Dorn like a burr. So much so that poor Dorn had no privacy. That woman trailed her everywhere and refused to leave her alone. Maybe Dorn went to a hotel or another inn for a while, just to get away from her."

"You think she might have?"

Logan's smile was tight and forced. "It's entirely possible. She wouldn't know that Francie has left."

"Dorn and I haven't seen eye to eye since we got here," Camille said, "and since meeting her in person, she's no one I'd consider a friend. But even so, I wouldn't want to see something happen to her. Let's hope she returns soon."

"You are a kind young woman, Camille. Exactly as you are online." They traded smiles, then Logan turned to Liz. "You know, Liz, you think like a writer. You see possibilities in a variety of circumstances. You could build some good stories. Maybe you should get together with Sadie and form your own writers club."

She shook her head. "As intriguing as that sounds, this inn and my friends take up most of my time. Maybe someday."

"Ah, the lament for the hopeful and magical Someday. I hear it often."

"I'm sure you do."

"Well, not everyone is as passionate about pen and ink as I am. And now, I need to get to work on my book. I daresay you should bury yourself in writing too, Camille. We came here to write, not solve mysteries." He turned to Liz. "Please let me know what you find out about this situation."

"Of course. I'll try reaching her again."

Rather than wait to see if she connected with Dorn, he nodded and gave her a thumbs-up. While there was something to be said for getting on with the day's business, his reaction to the events of that morning bothered Liz. His interest was stirred, but he didn't seem too worried. Certainly not enough for him to offer to help look for Dorn. It was almost as if whatever had happened to the woman was of no consequence to him.

The writers went to their own rooms, but Liz lingered in the hallway and dialed Dorn's number again. This time the phone didn't even ring, and the automated voice reminded her that Dorn didn't have a voice mail system.

Liz had reached the head of the stairs when Sarah called to her from the doorway of the Somewhere in Time Room.

"You might want to see this," she said.

A myriad of disturbing visions darted through Liz's mind, not the least of which was Dorn lying unconscious—or worse—on the floor. Liz's skin prickled as she approached the doorway. Sarah stepped aside so Liz could enter.

She took a deep breath, gathered her grit, and went inside. On the bed, in a small pile, were the silver-framed photo of Beans, Liz's mother's Bible, the crystal candy dish from Steve, Miriam's quilt, and a folded, lace-trimmed white pillowcase. Relief that there was no body made her knees weak for a minute.

Liz gazed at the items. "So this means Francie is the one who took them. I wonder why."

"Perhaps she had need of them." Sarah met her eyes, her expression mild.

The words were gentle and nonjudgmental, but Liz was not as willing to accept them as Sarah was. "If that was the case, then I wish she had come to me. And I hardly understand why she'd have need of my personal mementos. At any rate, have you found anything else that doesn't belong here?"

"Not yet."

Liz glanced around the room, remembering Francie's excitement about staying in it. "Poor Francie. What a sad life she has, always seeking approval, always wanting to fit in, always being rejected."

Sarah said nothing. Liz gathered the items and carried them

downstairs to their usual places. She put the pillowcase in a laundry basket in the utility room and went back into the kitchen.

"Liz?"

Liz turned at the sound of Mary Ann's voice.

Mary Ann narrowed her eyes as she examined Liz's face. "You look worried."

"I am," she admitted. "I'm worried about all of us—including you and Sadie—because something is happening that I can't explain or even understand."

Mary Ann pulled her to the table and sat her down. "I know you, Liz, and it's clear as crystal that you're holding something back." Liz said nothing. Mary Ann folded her arms. "You are not leaving this room until you come clean."

She hated to bring further unease to her friend, but said, "Have you seen Dorn this morning?"

"I haven't. Why? Is something wrong with her?"

"She didn't come down for breakfast. And when she didn't touch the tray I left outside her room, Logan opened her door. She isn't there, and it looks like she hasn't been there all night."

Mary Ann's eyes grew big. "Oh my. Do you think she went home?"

"I don't think so. Her things are still here. And I just saw her car outside."

"That doesn't sound good."

"No, it doesn't. Sounds like maybe she wasn't expecting to leave, doesn't it?"

"Sounds like . . ." Mary Ann swallowed hard. "Like maybe someone hurt her and left her somewhere—or worse."

They stared at each other, their faces mirroring dread and suspicion. Mary Ann had said exactly what was running through Liz's mind.

15

Sarah came into the kitchen. "Liz, I found this under the mattress while I was changing the sheets in the Somewhere in Time Room." She held out a folded sheet of lined notebook paper.

Mary Ann met Liz's eyes. "What is it?"

Liz unfolded the paper, and Sarah slipped out of the room, as if the page held secrets to which she shouldn't be privy.

Liz ran her eyes over the first few lines. "It's a story. I suppose Francie wrote it." She lifted her gaze to Mary Ann. "Shall I read this aloud?"

"Yes. Go ahead."

"The title is The Beautiful Princess. 'Once upon a time a lovely beautiful girl named Nancie with beautiful dark braids went to visit her wonderful friends in a lovely wonderful old house with many beautiful wonderful old clocks.'"

She looked up. "Francie definitely wrote this. It sounds like the other things she wrote and read to us."

She turned back to the story. "'Nancie stayed in a lovely room with a beautiful bed and many wonderful, soft pillows with beautiful white pillowcases. She wanted lovely pillowcases just like the beautiful white ones in her lovely room on the pretty bed, but the wonderful friendly innkeeper named Liza might not let her have one. Nancie was sad and unhappy. Her Big People friends were not always nice, even when she tried to be friendly. One of them was unwonderful and not lovely at all. Her name was Donna, and she was mean. She wore a yellow wig and spied on people when they were not looking. Nancie decided she did not like Donna after all. She thought it would be lovely if her mean friend named Donna went away. All night Nancie stood in the doorway of her lovely beautiful bedroom and thought of how she could make—'" Liz frowned and turned the page over. "That's all."

Mary Ann took the page and read it. She looked up, shaking her head. "There has to be more. She's thinking of how she can . . ." She swallowed hard. "Liz, I don't like this."

"Neither do I. Let's go see if we can find anything more."

They searched the wardrobe, every dresser drawer, every shelf, behind the curtains, and beneath the furniture. Together they hefted the mattress up a few inches, and Mary Ann let the weight of it rest against her shoulders as Liz stretched one arm beneath, seeking the next page of Francie's story. She straightened.

"Nothing."

Mary Ann lowered the mattress back into place. "Do you suppose she wrote the rest in a notebook or on her computer?" she asked as they remade the bed.

"It's possible." Liz paused, thinking. "It just occurred to me that, if she was swiping things from the sitting room, she might have been stashing something else in there, as a swap, hiding them like she hid this story. It's a silly notion, I know, but Francie did peculiar things, and when people do peculiar things, anything is possible."

"Then let's go look. In fact, she might have even hidden something in the quilt shop."

Mary Ann dashed into Sew Welcome and explained the situation to Sadie, who enthusiastically pitched in. Soon, though, it was apparent Francie had not hidden more pages to her story, or anything else. At least not where they could find them.

"Maybe she gave it to Logan or Camille," Sadie suggested when they met in the kitchen a few minutes later. "Logan told me she's slipped numerous poems and stories under his door while they've been here."

Liz poured each of them a coffee. "If she gave Logan her manuscripts, then she probably did the same to Dorn. She was so eager for the two of them to give appraisals of her stories, even though the critiques I heard were harsh. She seemed completely incapable of understanding them. I felt sorry for her."

"I hate to say it," Mary Ann said, "but if all of her writing is anything like what we just read, I can imagine how awful the stories are. And if she gets upset when she thinks someone doesn't like her work . . . well, you saw, Liz. She didn't hear a word I said about the quilting."

"She was so eager to please you, and when she didn't, she blocked out anything else."

"Poor woman. No wonder she writes strange stories. I suppose it's her way of communicating."

"You should talk to Logan," Sadie said. "Maybe he has some insight. And Camille's a sharp cookie."

Liz shot a glance toward the ceiling as if she could see into their rooms and watch them write. She knew an intrusion would not be welcome. "They're busy with the purpose of their retreat, which is writing. Before I interrupt them at work, I'm going to call Francie and see if I can get a straight answer out of her."

"I think you should," Mary Ann said.

"She might make up something and tell me what she thinks I want to hear instead of the truth."

"It's worth a shot at least."

"While you two try to figure out what's going on, I'll get back to the shop. Good luck." Sadie's expression was skeptical as she left the room.

Agnes answered Francie's cell phone, her voice clipped and cold.

"Hello, this is Liz, from the Olde Mansion Inn. I'd like to speak with Francie please."

"Absolutely not! My sister has been through quite enough, and she is not talking to anyone."

"But I need to ask her about a story she wrote while she was here."

"I'm sorry, but you can't. We're on our way home, and I've given her a nerve pill. She's sound asleep."

"Then I'll call back later or you can have her call—"

"Ms. Eckardt, please listen. It is going to take weeks for Francie to recover from this little . . . adventure she's been on. Please don't call me or her again." Agnes ended the call.

"Well, all right then," she said. "If Agnes doesn't want to talk to me, my next call will be to the chief."

Camille came into the kitchen waving her empty coffee cup. "Hey, Liz. Do you have more coffee?" She paused, and a quick curious frown passed over her features. "You look upset. Is this a bad time? I can go next door to the bakery."

"You don't need to do that." Liz got up. "I'll make a fresh pot. I think we all need it."

"Has Dorn returned yet?"

"Not yet. And she hasn't called or texted or anything."

Camille grimaced. "I don't like the sound of that. Surely if she were staying elsewhere she would have let someone know. Logan, if no one else."

"Maybe she hasn't had the opportunity to get in touch," Liz said, trying to convince herself as well as Camille. "Cell phone service often can be unreliable."

"Hey, hey!" Sadie hollered as she burst into the kitchen, waving her cell phone. "I was looking at the community updates on the city's online page. Listen to what I read just now. 'According to reliable sources, the Jane Doe who was found injured and unconscious at the Olde Mansion Inn on Thursday morning was apparently pushed down the staircase by an unknown assailant. The victim was again attacked Friday evening shortly after she regained consciousness in the hospital. It is unknown at this time if the same person was responsible for the second attack, but sources say it is likely.'" Sadie looked up. "What do you think of that?"

"Something has happened to Dorn, I'm sure of it." Camille's face was white.

"Let's not make that leap, and let's not panic," Liz said, though her own heart pounded thick and heavy with dread. "I'll try calling her again." Once again, though, the call did not go through.

"It's not even ringing, like her phone is off or her battery's dead." She tried four more times, and each time the line clicked and died. "Nothing."

"Or something is wrong that has nothing to do with her phone." Mary Ann's voice was flat.

Liz agreed, and felt queasy. She glanced at Camille, who stared back at her with wide eyes. Liz wondered if she should worry about the safety of her other guests, even with Francie gone. Perhaps the best thing would be for them to leave the inn before anything happened to either one.

Or was she overreacting? Dorn was abrasive, but driven, and completely devoted to her career. Maybe, as Logan had suggested, the woman had simply gone away for some private time to write.

"Liz?" Camille rubbed her pale throat with trembling fingers. "You were on your way to see that woman last night, and the next thing we knew you'd been unconscious on the ground with a head injury. Maybe someone was trying to stop you from going."

Camille had put into words the uneasy thoughts Liz had harbored for several hours. "I'm afraid you might be right. But why would anyone attack me?"

"That's what we need to figure out." The three women studied Liz as if she were on a witness stand.

"The woman was attacked first in your inn," Camille said. "The location might have something to do with whatever is spurring this person into action."

"I don't see why my inn would matter."

"Not the inn itself, maybe, but the people who are staying here. Namely us." Camille looked around uneasily, as if she expected a villain to be slinking around the kitchen.

"Let's try not to think that way just yet," said Liz. "If we start acting out of fear, we'll accomplish nothing."

"That's right," Mary Ann said. "Camille, has anyone bothered you or Logan, or made any threats, or treated you in a way that causes concern about your safety?" Mary Ann asked.

"No, not at all. Well, Francie's behavior was annoying, but she didn't do anything malicious to either of us."

"Since we know Francie truly is unstable . . ." Mary Ann said.

"She could be capable of anything," Sadie finished for her.

"But there's still nothing to prove she had anything to do with that woman in the hospital or me," said Liz. "As I've said several times already, she did not display any of the behaviors her sister mentioned would happen if she hadn't been taking her medicine."

"Then tell me this," Sadie said, shaking an index finger, "why wouldn't the sister let you talk to Francie when you called?"

"Because she had given her a sedative."

Sadie folded her arms and huffed. "Maybe she lied to you about that. In fact, maybe those people just made up Francie's weird symptoms to throw you off the track. That family seems to have trouble with the truth. In my opinion, she just didn't want you talking to Francie. And why? Because she knows Francie has been up to no good."

"Sadie has a good point, Liz," Camille said.

"I hate to think the worst, but I agree." Liz sighed. "It's time for me to call the chief about this."

Mary Ann got up and refilled their cups while Liz made the call. "Hi, Chief. It's Liz. There's been another situation here at the inn. It seems one of our guests may have gone missing."

"May have? When was she last seen?"

"Last night at the party."

"And what party was that?"

"A party for the four authors who are having a retreat here. Sadie invited a few of our friends to meet them." She filled him in about Francie, her actions and departure with her family, and a synopsis of the partially written story Sarah had found hidden in the Somewhere in Time Room.

"I've called Francie to see if she could explain what that story means and to ask if she might have told Dorn about her hurt feelings, but her sister refuses to let me talk to her."

"I see. But if the sister is Francie's guardian, and Francie is as fragile as you indicate, the woman has the right to keep you away from her."

"Don't you find that suspicious?"

"Let's just say I find it interesting."

Interesting. After everything she'd just told him, he merely found it "interesting." She liked the chief and had enormous respect for him, but in a situation like this he could be quite tedious. She decided to push a little harder.

"But in light of what I've told you, don't you find that Dorn's disappearance this morning—or last night—is too coincidental? I've tried calling her, but her phone doesn't ring, and she doesn't have a voice mail system. Something is wrong, Stan."

She frowned when he kept her waiting for a response. She hoped the prolonged silence meant he was taking notes, or reading notes, or dispatching someone to look into this matter.

"I understand your concern," he said at last, "but she has been gone less than twenty-four hours. Let's give her a few more hours to turn up. She's a grown woman on a vacation, and in all likelihood has decided to abandon the retreat for a time."

Liz decided to try another approach. "I've thought of that. But according to an update on the city's online news page this morning, the woman in the hospital was deliberately shoved down the staircase here at the inn."

Another brief silence. This time she imagined his back stiffening and a disapproving scowl digging into his face.

"That information is online?" he growled.

"Yes. We discussed the possibility, remember? Is it definite?"

He huffed. "Liz, you know you can't believe everything you read on the Internet. At least you *should* know that."

"Of course I know that. Come *on*. I gave you the latest information I had. Can't you extend the same courtesy? Isn't that what we agreed to when I was in your office?"

He blew out another long, noisy breath. "Let me put it this way. I am not going to deny the story you read."

"And don't you think that whoever it was that attacked her in the hospital room is more than likely the same person who pushed her down the stairs?"

"It would seem that way."

"And don't you think it is entirely possible that the same person knocked me out last night?"

"What? Repeat that." Liz now imagined him leaning forward in his chair, hand clenched around the phone, his frown deeper than ever, his mind bristling with fresh interest.

"I went outside last night, and I think someone attacked me near the garage."

"You *think* someone attacked you?" he nearly yelled. "Don't you *know*?"

"It was dark and rainy, so when I came to, I thought I had fallen and hit my head on something. I don't remember clearly what actually happened. The doctor who examined me said there is an oblong-shaped bruise on the side of my head. So considering everything else, I'm not so sure I did fall. I think someone might have clobbered me."

The three women at the kitchen table had yet to take their eyes off her.

"Was anyone else around when this happened?"

"No, I was alone."

"Was this before or after the party?"

"During."

"So, if you were having a party at the inn last night, why were you outside in the dark, in the rain, all alone?"

"I was going to my car."

"And where were you going?"

"To the hospital, to see about that woman. But what's important is that Francie Sloan left the party early, someone got to me, someone got to that woman in the hospital, and now Dorn Alexander is missing. I'm afraid someone got to her too."

There was another brief silence, then he asked, "I will see to it that someone contacts Ms. Sloan and her family. Now give me the names of everyone who was at that party."

This conversation was not going the way she had expected or wanted it to. She most certainly did not want any of her friends to be interrogated by the police—although this wouldn't be the first time—but it sounded like that was exactly what the chief planned to do.

He's just doing his job, she reminded herself. She told him what he wanted to know.

"But what about Dorn?" she asked after she delivered the final name.

"If she fails to call or show up by this evening, let me know," he said. "If you think of anything more, call me. And, Liz?" His voice softened. "Please take care of yourself. Be watchful. Okay?"

Her tension eased a bit, and she couldn't stop the little smile that came to her lips. He was a good man, and she was grateful that he cared.

"Yes, okay. I will do that. Thanks, Stan."

16

By late afternoon, Dorn had neither called nor shown up.

When Liz had gotten off the phone with Chief Houghton that morning, she tried to ease the minds of the three women at the kitchen table.

"You need to get back to your writing, Camille," she said. "You don't want to let this time go to waste." She turned to Sadie and Mary Ann. "And you two should be tending to Sew Welcome. What if someone has come in and we didn't notice? You might have lost customers."

"We closed the shop for a bit," Sadie said. "Some things are more important."

"That's right," Mary Ann said. "Are you all right, Liz? Can we do anything for you before we go back to the shop?"

"No. The best thing any of you can do for me is to return to your regular routine. I plan to do some baking today, and I'm giving Sarah the rest of the day off so I'll have the kitchen to myself. I need to think." She refused to tell them she wanted the young woman home with her husband and family, safe and sound.

True to her word, she did her best to keep busy. She tried to stop worrying, but throughout the day her concerns continued to rear their heads, pointing out what-ifs at every turn. The chief didn't call with any updates.

Logan came downstairs, freshly showered, shaved, and smelling of his signature cologne. Liz was in the kitchen, making fudge frosting for a fresh pan of brownies on the cooling rack.

"Look at you," she said with a smile. "Dressed up for any special reason?"

He smiled. "Sadie and I are going out for dinner to a place she likes in Bertram. I believe that's a small town not far from Pleasant Creek."

"Not too far. I hope you have a good time."

"We will. Sadie is a special woman."

"Yes, she is." She paused and held his gaze. "She's a loving, giving woman. I'd hate for anyone to hurt her."

"Ah, Liz. Please don't concern yourself on that account. Sadie and I know where each other stands, and we're all right with it."

"You'll be gone soon, though."

"Yes, that's true. But I won't be out of her life. We've made a good connection, and I think a solid friendship is developing. Please don't worry. I would never hurt Sadie."

Liz wanted to say more, to tell him she knew about his many romantic conquests and failed commitments, but she recalled Sadie's words from their earlier conversation. She held her peace, but she also said a silent prayer that her friend's heart would be safe.

"Since Dorn hasn't returned, I thought it was time to give you this." He handed her a small piece of paper with a phone number scrawled on it. "This is Dorn's home phone number."

Her mouth flew open, and she wiped a stray bit of frosting off her fingers onto a paper towel before taking it from him.

"Why didn't you give this to me earlier?"

"Because when she gave me that number last year, it was with the solemn promise that I would never share it with anyone. And until now, I haven't. I hate breaking my word, but since she has not returned, I think it's time to make the call. Maybe she's gone home."

"But if you have had this number all this time, then why didn't you call before now? That wouldn't have been breaking your word." Did he have an agenda she failed to understand?

"Honestly, I thought she was just playing hooky from the retreat.

Getting away from Francie, for one thing, but for another, getting away from Camille and me."

She frowned. "I thought you were close friends."

He shook his head. "Only online. As you probably know, friendships formed online don't always work out once the parties meet in person. I think this is the case with Dorn. Now, Camille and I get along quite well. We have a connection like a father and daughter." He smiled. "That girl is gold. But as for Dorn leaving to get away from us, I believe her feelings are wounded because of our reaction to the manuscript she's been sharing. It has been far below her usual high standards. Camille and I have both mentioned it to her, and I have even tried to talk to her about it privately. But she's been both resistant to suggestions and angry that we aren't thrilled with her new style or genre. So my thoughts have been that she's gone off to sulk and nurse her wounded ego."

"Maybe so, but I still think trying to get in touch with her would be wise. If she's gone home to pout, at least we can put our minds at rest."

"You really are worried, aren't you?"

"After what happened to the unknown woman and me, and after what we learned about Francie? You bet I am."

"Then it's time to lay your worries to rest." He started to take his phone from the inner pocket of his jacket, then paused. "Do you want to make the call, or shall I?"

"I'll call," she said. "If she's angry at you, she might not talk."

He tapped his temple and nodded. "Good thinking. And I'll go see if Sadie is ready for our date."

Liz wondered if Sadie thought of it as a date. She mentally shook her head. If anyone could take care of herself, it was Sadie.

Liz went to her quarters to make the call. She wanted to sit in solitude for a bit and tamp down the negative emotions that had been churning like dark waters within her all day. Those thoughts had served no purpose other than to occupy her mind. She needed to be clearheaded and calm when she talked with Dorn.

Taking a deep breath, she entered the number, and as it rang offered up a quick prayer. *Please, let her be home.*

"Alexander residence. Billy speaking." The voice had a distinctive and cultured Southern drawl.

"Hello. May I please speak to Dorn?"

"I'm sorry, ma'am, but Dorn is at a retreat for writers this week. I'm her husband. May I take a message?"

Her husband? What was she supposed to say to a husband about his possibly missing wife? Words stuck in Liz's throat.

"I . . . that is, have you heard from her recently?"

"She's texted me a few times. Why? Is something wrong?"

"Uh . . ." Liz gathered her wits quickly. "I found her diabetes medication and wondered if—"

"There must be a mistake. She doesn't have diabetes, and she doesn't take any medication. She tries to keep healthy through eating mostly natural foods. You've found someone else's medication."

"Apparently so." What did this mean? "Can you tell me when you last texted with her?"

"Just a few minutes ago. She said she was having a great time, the writers were fabulous, and she might stay in Indiana a little longer. If you need to leave a message . . ."

She swallowed hard. There was no way she was going to alarm this man until she had more time to think through the situation. If something dire had happened to Dorn, the authorities needed to be the ones to let him know.

"Thanks, but I'll call back later. Goodbye."

She hung up and flopped back against the sofa, heart thundering. For a few seconds, she sprawled there, staring at the ceiling while trying to catch her breath and gather her wits.

She needed to talk to the others.

Logan and Sadie were just going out the front door as Liz hurried toward the quilt shop. Sadie was dressed in a hot-pink knit top with beige pants.

"Has Mary Ann left yet? I need to talk to all of you," Liz said.

"What on earth . . . ? Liz, you look awful." Sadie grabbed her arm as if she thought Liz might pass out. "Let's go into the shop. You sit down."

Beans followed, staying close to Liz. She sat, and when he pressed against her leg, she stroked his broad head.

"Logan, would you please go get Camille and ask her to join us?" Liz asked.

"Of course."

"What's wrong?" Mary Ann said. "Liz, are you ill?"

"I'm fine, but we need to discuss this situation and decide what to do."

"Situation?"

"Yes. The unknown woman. Francie. Dorn. Me." She pointed to the injured side of her head that was now spurting pain like fiery bullets with every heartbeat.

Sadie hurried out of the room and returned with a glass of water.

"Here. Take a few sips, then some deep breaths." She glanced behind her. "Here are Logan and Camille."

She pulled up chairs for them and everyone sat down, eyeing Liz with considerable concern.

"What's going on?" Sadie prompted. "You look green."

"I feel green. And I wish I knew what was going on."

"Well, then, tell us what you *do* know," Logan said. "You made the call to Dorn's house?"

"Yes. Just a few minutes ago."

"And?"

"And her husband answered."

"And?" Sadie twitched impatiently.

Liz took another drink of water. "And he said she had sent him a text earlier today, just a little bit ago, in fact, saying she was having a great time at the retreat and she planned to stay longer than she originally thought."

Cries of shock and confusion filled the shop.

"But how?" Sadie spluttered. "She's not here!"

Liz tried not to look at her in exasperation, but failed. "That's why I want to talk to all of you. We need to figure out what's happening."

"Have you called Stan?" Mary Ann asked.

"Not yet."

"Maybe she's just keeping a low profile," Mary Ann suggested. "She doesn't want to go home yet, but she doesn't want to be here."

Liz wished she could believe that Dorn had simply locked herself away in another hotel and was busily writing her book.

"When I mentioned her diabetes medicine, her husband said she doesn't have diabetes. That she's more or less a health nut."

"She didn't strike me as a health nut," Sadie said. "She ate a lot of cookies and cake at the party, and she drank a lot of coffee. Health nuts don't do that."

"Something isn't right," Liz declared. "We need to get to the bottom of this situation, and I think if we put our heads together, we can."

"I agree with you," Logan said. "We are all smart people in this room, and we've all seen some of what's happening firsthand. We need to share our knowledge and discuss the facts with open minds. Let's start at the beginning."

"Which was when that woman fell down the stairs," Sadie said.

Logan shook his head. "But that is not the beginning."

"Then what is?" Sadie asked.

"Whatever happened before she got here."

"We have no idea what happened to her before she got here," Liz said. "We don't even know why she was here in the first place."

"Well, it's a cinch that someone did not like her," Sadie said.

"Or maybe she surprised someone who wasn't supposed to be here," Camille said. "If I remember correctly, she showed up early and no one was in the inn."

"That's right." Liz nodded. "I went next door to get pastries for everyone that morning."

"And we came to the shop earlier than usual, but went for a walk," Mary Ann said.

"If we hadn't, none of this would have happened." Sadie's shoulders rounded and she sighed deeply.

"Oh, you can't blame yourself, Sadie," Liz said.

"It's the truth! We should have been more attentive and realized that neither you nor Sarah were here. If we hadn't been arguing about those Burgess sisters, we wouldn't have felt the need to go clear our heads by taking a walk. And if we had locked—"

"Stop it." Camille gave her a stern look. "Your earlier-than-usual arrival and the argument about the Burgess sisters have nothing to do with this."

"That's right, Sadie," Liz said. "We can blame ourselves all day long for certain actions, but that gets us nowhere. Let's focus on what we know."

"And that is?"

"An unknown person was found here in the inn after being pushed down the stairs."

"And how do we know she was pushed down the stairs?" Sadie leaned forward as if imparting great news. "Because there were bruises on her body that said so."

"How do you know that?" Camille said.

Sadie shot an uneasy glance at Liz and Mary Ann.

Liz jumped in. "Because the police confirmed it. At least the chief didn't deny it, which I consider confirmation."

"But we still don't know the identity of the woman," Mary Ann added, "or why she was here. She'd made no reservations. Right, Liz?"

"Right. She may have been a walk-in, but that is rare so early in the morning. If someone wants to stay overnight in an inn or hotel, they usually travel awhile to get there, and then spend the night. I don't see it happening near sunrise." She shook her head.

"Okay, so we know she travels early," Logan said. "But that could just mean she's what my mother would've called a 'go-getter.'"

"But do we know anything about the person who shoved her?" Mary Ann asked.

"Nothing." Liz shrugged. "But if that person was here as early as she was, then maybe that person is a go-getter too."

"Or maybe that person traveled with her," Camille said.

"That's very likely," Liz said, "but since we don't know the victim, how can we know who traveled with her?"

"We can't. Not yet, anyway." Logan swept his gaze across Liz, Sadie, and Mary Ann. "Have there been any break-ins or thefts in this area lately?"

"Not that I've heard anything about," Liz said.

"Nor me," Mary Ann said.

"And if there had been," Sadie said, "you'd better believe Rob Carver would have written it up as the biggest crime wave ever to hit the Midwest."

"Rob Carver?" Interest gleamed in Camille's bright eyes. "You mean that cute red-haired reporter who was asking a lot of questions at the party?"

"Cute?" Sadie wrinkled her nose as if she smelled something rotten. "If you don't care who you call cute, then yes, that was him. Making a regular pest of himself as usual. If that boy can't find dirt to write about, he'll go dig it up in the garden."

"Oh, Sadie," Mary Ann laughed. "He's just eager to get a big break."

"No, he's a nosy busybody who likes to stir things up."

"Let's get back to the subject at hand," Logan said with a smile at Sadie. "We know someone else was in this inn that morning. Think back a minute, Liz. Did you notice anything that was different from what you normally see or hear or smell?"

She thought about it, then shook her head. "If so, it wasn't significant enough for me to remember it."

"What about between here and the bakery? Did you see anything unusual that caught your eye? Maybe someone you didn't know lingering outside as if watching or waiting for someone?"

"No, the wind was blowing so hard that morning that I pretty much kept my head down instead of looking around. Besides, my mind was focused on the arrival of you writers. I was hoping your retreat would be everything you wanted it to be."

"It has certainly been an unforgettable experience," Camille said, "and it's getting more memorable by the minute. But you and your inn are lovely."

"And while you were at the bakery?" Logan prompted.

"Did I notice anything or anyone unusual there? Not really. But again, my mind was on other things, and I wasn't checking for oddities."

"How long were you there?"

"Not long. Maybe twenty minutes. Probably less. Naomi and I had a little chat over coffee and a couple of doughnuts. She always has a lot of customers coming in, especially in the mornings. We should ask her if she noticed anyone acting suspiciously."

"I'll do it!" Sadie said, raising her hand as if she were volunteering to clap erasers. Her eagerness made Liz frown. Was it just her natural inclination to take the bull by the horns and get things done, or was Sadie trying to please Logan?

"Not just yet." He gave her another friendly smile. "You said Sarah was the one who found this woman?"

"Right."

"But she wasn't here when you left?"

"No one was here when I left. I would have heard her in the kitchen, since she usually comes in through the utility room door."

He looked at Mary Ann. "The woman was not at the foot of the stairs when you got to the quilt shop?"

"No, and we would have seen her when we opened up."

"She was pretty hard to miss," Sadie said.

"And you were sure Sarah wasn't here at the time?"

"I didn't see or hear her," Sadie replied. "I just assumed."

Mary Ann shook her head. "Logan, this is a big house. Even if Sarah *had* been on the third floor or in the four-season room, it's perfectly reasonable that she didn't hear anything."

"Hmm." Logan's eyes narrowed in thought.

"If you're considering that Sarah might have had anything to do with any of this," Liz said sharply, "you couldn't be further from the truth."

"I should say so!" Sadie glared at him. "Surely you don't think that sweet young girl could do anything as awful as push a stranger down the stairs or stab her in the hospital or attack Liz."

He held up a hand. "I never said a word against her. I'm sure she's a good and peace-loving young woman—"

"Yes, she is, so don't even *think* about making her into one of your suspects." Sadie folded her arms and stared him down.

"All right. Okay. We'll leave Sarah out of it for now, although I think we should talk to her about what she might have heard or seen before she found the woman."

"The police have already talked with her," Liz said.

"I'm sure they have, but maybe she'd be apt to remember more if she talked with one of her friends instead."

"I'll talk to her tomorrow if need be," Liz said. "In the meantime, we're pretty sure there was no one in or around the inn who was memorable in any way."

"That you know of," he said firmly.

"Right."

"Maybe someone you know broke in," Camille said. "Someone who knows when there is most likely to be no one inside and would know what time the quilt shop opens and what time Sarah comes to work."

"All valid points, my dear," Logan said, nodding. "Thank you."

"I think it is quite possible that someone, most likely Francie, was upstairs, looking for me," Liz said, "and this woman simply came in and surprised her."

"Enough to shove the woman down the stairs?" Camille shook her head.

"Maybe she didn't mean to shove her down the staircase," Mary Ann said. "Maybe she just reacted."

"But that doesn't explain the other two attacks," Logan pointed out.

Mary Ann sighed. "No, you're right. It doesn't. So what does?"

The short silence fell while each of them pursued their own thoughts for a time. Without conscious volition, Liz found herself gazing at Camille, so bright-eyed and eager to solve this mystery. An unwelcome reminder crept into her mind, telling her that Camille had behaved suspiciously more than once since her arrival. She had gone into rooms on the third floor when she had no reason to.

She had picked up items on various shelves in the inn, examining them as if appraising their resale value. And Liz had found her in the kitchen, in the dark, rummaging through a cupboard. But as unsettling as these activities had been, none of them proved anything more than that she was snoopy or somnambulistic, or both.

The more Liz thought about it, though, the more she wondered if it was possible the young woman had taken the items from the sitting room, then later planted them in Francie's room to throw suspicion onto her. Had her foray into the kitchen in the middle of the night been something other than sleepwalking?

How long had Camille been in town before she came to the inn? Could her eager young author act be nothing more than that—an act? But what reason could she have for sneaking into the inn? Was it possible she knew the woman in the hospital and had slipped away from the party last night to cause her further harm?

Oh, surely not!

But she certainly had seemed fascinated by the staircase and the newel post when she first arrived. Why had she shown such interest in the very places where blood had been spilled?

"Let's move on, shall we?" Logan interrupted her thoughts. He turned to her. "Liz, what do we know about the woman in the hospital?"

"Not much. As far as I know, she remains unidentified, unless she said something yesterday after she woke up."

"Excuse me." Camille abruptly left the room.

Everyone stared after her, except Logan. He tapped his pen against his chin as he gazed at Liz as if he were trying to get inside some locked bit of information she knew but withheld. The very notion rankled her.

"Tell me what that woman looks like," he said to her.

"I beg your pardon?"

"The woman at the foot of the staircase. Tell me what she looks like."

She lifted both hands in a helpless gesture. "I can't do that."

"You can try, can't you?"

"It won't be accurate, because she was facedown at the foot of the stairs."

"Then give me your impression of what she looked like."

This seemed an exercise in futility, but she figured Logan had a reason for asking her to do this, and if it would help, even a little bit, she would try to tell him what he wanted to know.

"I'd say she was tall, wouldn't you?" She looked at Mary Ann and Sadie.

"Tall, yes," Mary Ann said. "Long-legged. Maybe five-ten or so."

"And slender," Sadie added.

"She was well-dressed," Liz said, surprised that she could recall the violet trousers and black blouse the woman wore. "Her face was pretty battered, but I took her pulse and now that I think about it, her skin was quite smooth and rather pale."

Odd how little details she hadn't remembered came into her mind.

"So would you say she was young?"

"Not as young as Camille, but probably in her late thirties. And she had blonde hair."

"The hairstyle," Sadie said. "Don't forget that." Before Liz could say a word, she turned to Logan. "She had a terrible hairdo. I know it's trendy to have a spiky style, and I know taking a tumble down the stairs can mess up a person's hair, but hers looked . . ." She gestured helplessly.

"As if someone had hacked it off?"

Her eyes rounded. "Exactly. How'd you know that?"

"I was just speculating, and the idea seemed to fit."

According to Caitlyn, the woman's hair *had* been hacked off. But Liz hadn't shared that information with anyone, and Liz hadn't seen it in the newspaper. So how could Logan make that assumption?

Unless he had seen her—or done it to her.

17

Sadie stared at Logan with open admiration. "That's why you're such a famous mystery writer. You speculate." She winked and tapped her index finger against her temple. "And your ideas seem to fit."

"That's kind of you to say, but really, it's just a matter of thought and deduction."

She waved one hand dismissively. "You are gifted, Logan Tracy, admit it. And I should know, because I am your number-one fan."

"Yes, I know." He chuckled.

Mary Ann cleared her throat. Sadie glanced at her, then pressed her lips together as if indicating she would try not to get off track again.

"Any birthmarks or tattoos that you noticed?" Logan asked, all business again.

"I didn't see any," Liz said, watching Logan carefully. The theory about the unknown woman being one of Logan's romantic conquests—though not the most recent one, Madison—came to roost in her mind.

"Me either," Mary Ann said.

"Nor me," Sadie added.

"Was she wearing jewelry?"

Liz shook off her thoughts for the moment, trying to remember. "I don't think so. Maybe a wedding ring, but I can't be sure. Her jewelry, birthmarks, or tattoos were not on my mind. Her survival was."

"I understand that, Liz, but what we're trying to do here is to jog your memory." He got up and paced a few steps as if pacing helped him to think. After a bit, he turned to her.

"Let's try something different that often works in a situation like this."

"What is it?"

"I know you don't think you remember much, but I want you to try to draw a good, detailed picture in your mind of what do you remember about her. Will you do that?"

"I'll try, but I don't know how . . ."

He came and stood next to her, looking earnestly down into her face. "This might sound a little strange to you, but it usually works, so trust me, okay? The first step is to close your eyes so that you don't see everything around you. This well help your concentration."

She closed her eyes.

"Now, take a deep breath and blow it out slowly, and as you do, try to block out everything else."

"All right." She did as he asked, breathing deeply and exhaling.

"Are you trying to hypnotize her?" Sadie's loud voice carried a heavy thread of indignation, and Liz's eyes popped open to see the woman glaring at her idol. "Because, if you are, I—"

Logan frowned at her. "Sadie, please. I'm just helping Liz remember and visualize what she saw."

"She won't be clucking like a chicken when it's over, will she?"

"What?"

"Oh, for heaven's sake," Mary Ann said. "Sadie, why don't you go get everyone some coffee? Make yours decaf."

Sadie put up both hands in surrender. "I won't say another word."

"This is not hypnotism," Logan assured her. "If it was, I'd tell you. This won't hurt Liz in any way. In fact, I often use this technique on myself when I'm visualizing a vital scene in my books."

Sadie nodded, waving one hand back and forth as if shooing away a fly. "All right. I'll mind my own business."

"Thank you." He gave her a smile, then turned back to Liz. "Let's start over. Close your eyes and take a few deep breaths, trying to block out all the sights and sounds around you." She closed her eyes again and followed his suggestion. He lowered his voice to a near whisper as he added, "Now. Set your mind on the woman who fell. See her in your memory as clearly as you can. And as you do that, see if there is anything at all, even some little something, you can recall."

She concentrated on bringing that morning back into her memory with as much detail as possible. Had it only been the day before yesterday? Surely it would be easy to remember everything. But no matter how hard she tried to see something new, nothing surfaced in her memory.

After a while, she shook her head and opened her eyes. "I'm sorry. I'm afraid I have told you all I can remember."

"It's okay. You've done fine. It was worth a try." He returned to his chair and tilted his head to one side as he looked at her. "Do you still have that image of her in your mind?"

"Oh, yes, but I wish I didn't. I don't like thinking of it."

"That is completely understandable. But if you can just keep it there for a little longer, that would be helpful."

"Do I need to close my eyes again?"

"Not this time, unless you'd like to." He smiled. "Does that woman resemble anyone you know?"

"I know willowy blondes here in town. Patsy Reynolds, one of the checkout clerks at the local supermarket, for instance. And the high school principal's assistant, but I've forgotten her name."

"Don't forget Simone at the nail salon," Sadie piped up. "I don't know her last name. Do you, Mary Ann?"

"Fletcher." Mary Ann turned to Logan. "Why are we doing this? If that woman was anyone local, don't you think her family would have reported it and identified her by now?"

"One would think so, but I want us to cover every contingency, no matter how trite or how extreme."

Camille came back into the room, carrying a cup of coffee.

"I made fresh coffee for everyone. I hope that was okay." As she sat down, she nursed a tiny smile, as if she bore a secret.

"Of course. Thank you." Liz turned to Logan. "I hardly think it's likely that she is someone local. No one asked me, but it seems the wiser thing would be to leave the identifying of her to the authorities and concentrate our efforts on finding out who assaulted that poor woman. After all, the police have the resources and opportunities we do not."

Logan gave her a strained smile. "You have a point, but my point has been that if she is anyone you or your friends know, we might be able to ferret out a list of people who had reason to hurt her."

"That's a long shot, though, isn't it?" Sadie asked.

He sat back, nodding. "Yes, it is, unfortunately. Amateur investigation doesn't work as well in real life as it does in fiction."

"Amateur is pretty much all we have right now," Camille said. "So let's make use of our powers of deduction, although none of us are as gifted as Sherlock Holmes."

"Logan is!" Sadie said stoutly.

"No, I'm not," he insisted. "I wish I were." He gave her a rueful smile and patted her hand.

"I will believe what I want to believe." Sadie folded her arms and set her chin. "So that's that."

Everyone laughed a little, then Camille turned back to the subject at hand.

"We know that there was no purse, wallet, or phone with her, nothing to identify who she is or where she comes from. So it stands to reason those things were stolen, along with her jewelry. If she had any."

"I think you are absolutely right," Liz said. "She's someone who, despite her injuries, looked as if she took good care of herself. Her clothes seemed to be high quality, maybe even designer, and someone like that would wear good jewelry."

Mary Ann said. "She would probably carry an expensive handbag."

"With plenty of credit cards," Sadie added. "And I think she'd wear designer shoes, but she was barefoot."

Liz said. "The chief and I searched the inn but found nothing that might have belonged to her. Whoever assaulted her took all her things except the clothes she was wearing."

Camille passed around a look. "And this leads us right back to Francie, who took items from the sitting room."

Liz met the younger woman's eyes. A flicker of something flashed across Camille's expression and she looked away, sipping her coffee. Camille was a sleepwalker and picked up items during her jaunts. Had she accumulated the items and, out of embarrassment, blamed the thefts on poor Francie?

"How did you know items went missing from the sitting room?" Liz asked. "I never mentioned it to you."

A rosy tinge colored Camille's cheeks. "I, uh, I tend to . . . overhear things."

Sadie narrowed her eyes. "You mean eavesdrop?"

"If you want to call it that, then, yes, I do." She gave the group a defiant look. "I am curious by nature and—"

"And snoopy by choice?"

"Sadie!" Mary Ann frowned at her.

"I am interested in what goes on around me," Camille said. "And I try to store it all up here." She tapped the side of her head. "These bits and pieces that I gather from life experiences and from my surroundings will enrich my writing. I hope."

"Of course they will," Logan said. "But we're off track again. We are not here to dissect Camille's approach or question her inquiring mind. We are here to try to solve the mystery at this inn. Let's return to what we know, shall we?" He looked at Liz. "Did Francie swipe items from the sitting room or didn't she?"

"It seems so, yes. I noticed yesterday that some small things had gone missing from the sitting room. Nothing had much monetary value except the small silver picture frame, but everything taken carried a lot of sentimental value to me. I really hated to lose them because some of them were irreplaceable. However, after Francie left, we found everything on her bed, plus another item."

"What else?" Logan asked.

"A pillowcase from the Somewhere in Time Room."

Camille's forehead wrinkled. "A pillowcase? That seems peculiar. But look who we're talking about. Francie was nothing but peculiar."

"Did anything else go missing from the inn or from the quilt shop?" Logan asked.

"Nothing has been taken from Sew Welcome," Mary Ann said.

"I don't think anything else is missing from the inn," Liz said, "but I wonder if she took anything that belonged to either of you or Dorn."

"Not that I've noticed," Camille said.

"I thought I'd brought one more book than I did," Logan said, "but maybe I miscounted. Dorn never mentioned anything missing from her room."

"Except her," Liz said.

"Right. Except her."

Mary Ann stirred. "Tell them about the story, Liz. Something about it just now clicked in my mind."

Logan frowned. "Story? What story?"

"Something Francie left in her room, which Sarah found today."

"Not just left it," Mary Ann corrected. "Francie had hidden it beneath the mattress. And in my opinion her strange little tale is . . . well, cryptic. Rather frightening, in fact."

Logan's expression darkened, giving him a forbidding expression. "Why didn't you mention this earlier?" he asked Liz.

Next to her, Beans jolted awake. He growled deep in his throat and looked toward the doorway. A moment later, the front door opened and approaching firm footsteps sounded against the floor. Rob Carver swaggered in. The grin on his face might have been construed as a smirk.

Beans stood and barked at him.

Rob stopped grinning.

"Hush, Beans," Liz said. She placed her hand on his muscular side, felt his tension. "Easy, now. Good boy."

Grumbling, the bulldog settled back to the floor beside her, but he stayed wide awake, watching Rob.

"What are you doing here?" Sadie gawked at him as if a muddy horse had just galloped through Sew Welcome.

His eyes went straight to Camille, who pulled up a chair from one of the sewing machines and put it next to her.

"I called him a few minutes ago and asked him to come over," she said as he sat beside her.

"Why did you do that?" Sadie demanded.

"Because maybe he can help us."

Sadie snorted.

"Rob was at the party," Camille said. "He took pictures and talked to a lot of people, not just us writers. He might have some information we can use."

"Who knows?" he said, a hint of a smirk once again on his face. "I might."

Sadie scowled and tapped one foot. "Maybe."

The reporter never seemed to mind digging in places where he had no business. Doing so *was* his business after all, but he approached it with bluster and steel. In a small town like Pleasant Creek, a dark story could cast a pall over the entire community. Very few people trusted Rob Carver. Not because he told untruths, but because he didn't care who he plowed over to get whatever juicy tidbits he might unearth. While Liz understood Sadie's annoyance, she also agreed with Camille. The man might very well have some information that would help them.

"Good. We will tap into your knowledge soon, Mr. Carver," Logan said "But first, let's get back to what we were talking about before this young man showed up. Liz, you seemed reluctant to mention the story Francie wrote. Was there a reason you wanted to keep it to yourself?"

"Of course not. I had every intention of talking to you about it, and now I am. It's one of the reasons I wanted us to meet." She pulled the handwritten page from her pocket and opened it, smoothing the folds. She looked at Logan. "Shall I read this to you or would you rather read it yourself?"

"Go ahead. Please."

She turned to Rob. "You do understand that nothing about any of this is to go in your newspaper, don't you?"

He merely met her eyes.

"I'm serious, Rob. If you don't think you can participate off the record, then you'll have to leave."

Camille laid one hand on his forearm and smiled at him. She held his gaze as she said, "We really need your help, so you'll do as Liz asked, won't you?"

A flush stole up his neck as her pretty face and bright eyes wound him securely around her little finger. Liz suppressed a grin.

"Sure. I'll keep it off the record." He looked at Liz. "But when your little puzzle is solved, I want to get the details—all the details.

Everyone in town knows the woman was targeted here and in the hospital, so they are not only curious but they're uneasy that someone seems to have an ax to grind. I'd like to help put their minds at rest."

Sadie rolled her eyes. "This situation has nothing to do with the townspeople. It's perfectly obvious she has targeted Liz and the writers."

"I assume 'she' is Francie Sloan?" Rob said.

"Right."

"I thought she was a few bricks short of a load when I talked to her. Talking about fairies and elves as if they were real people." He lifted one eyebrow. "I mean, really."

"Let's see what this story contains," Logan said. "Go ahead and read it, my dear."

Liz read the partial story to them. "And that's where it ends."

"What?" Rob looked around as if he thought another explanation would be forthcoming from the others. "A kid wrote that, surely."

"Nope, that's all Francie," Logan replied.

"Where's the rest of it?"

"We don't know," Liz said. "Maybe she took it with her. Maybe she never wrote more of it."

"If she hid that," he said, pointing at the page, "then maybe she hid more."

"We looked everywhere for it."

Liz turned to Mary Ann. "You said something about this clicked in your mind?"

She nodded. "Reread the part about Donna."

"'Her name was Donna, and she was mean. She wore a yellow wig and spied on people when they were not looking. Nancie decided she did not like Donna after all. She thought it would be lovely if her mean friend named Donna went away. All night Nancie stood in the doorway of her lovely beautiful bedroom and thought of how she could make—'" Liz looked up.

"Since she barely disguised the characters in her story, it must be set here at the inn. Nancie is Francie, and Donna is obviously Dorn." Mary Ann looked at the others. "Wouldn't you concur?"

"That's entirely logical," Logan said, and the others murmured in agreement.

The front door opened, and Caitlyn appeared in the quilt shop doorway. She was in her scrubs and hospital shoes. She seemed understandably surprised when she saw the group sitting in a cluster in the middle of Sew Welcome.

"What's going on?"

"Come join us, Caitlyn," Liz said. "We're trying to sort out the events of the last few days."

"Making any progress?" she asked as she inserted a chair next to Liz and sat down.

"I don't know about anyone else, but the more we talk about it, the more confused I get," Sadie said. "We still don't know anything about that woman in the hospital, or if Francie or someone else is responsible for her injuries and Liz's. Or what her story means, or what has happened to Dorn. We've been mulling it over for a while, but I don't know if we're any closer to the answers than we were when we started."

"Well, let me either confuse you even more or add a little clarity," Caitlyn said. "I heard about the footage from our security cameras last night."

"You mean there's footage with the person who attacked that woman?" Mary Ann asked.

Caitlyn nodded. "I haven't seen it, but I did a little asking around and talked to someone who had seen it."

"And?" Liz leaned forward, her heart beating fast.

"There was someone seen going into the woman's hospital room. Then there was a lot of noise, and the person who went into the room fled."

"Did they see what this person looked like?"

She shook her head. "Gender is undetermined because of bulky clothing, but someone about five-eight, frizzy gray hair, walking with a decided limp."

"That's it?" Liz leaned forward. *A limp?* "What about the face? What about the age?"

"Closed-circuit television doesn't always give a good clear picture. And the gray hair would indicate this person is older."

"And they know this is the person who pushed the woman down the staircase?"

Caitlyn shook her head. "I have no idea, but I do know this is their best possible suspect."

"Francie is tiny," Mary Ann said. "Even if she wore a gray wig and faked a limp, there is no way she could fake eight inches in height."

"That's right. So we really must rule her out as a suspect," Logan observed. "At least for the stabbing."

"But she's the best one we have!" Sadie said. She ticked off points on her fingers. "Unbalanced mental state, peculiar behavior and reactions, thievery. And that weird little story in which Nancie wants to get rid of Donna. Maybe she had platform shoes and wore a wig."

"Wigs," Liz murmured as bits and pieces began to gather from the corners of her mind. "Donna wears a yellow wig." She looked at the story in her hand.

"And isn't nice to her friends," Mary Ann added.

"A yellow wig," Liz repeated. "Dorn's blonde hair is peculiar, to say the least."

"I betcha it's a wig!" Sadie said.

"And Dorn uses a cane—which suggests she might have a limp," Liz said. Was it possible that Dorn had done this? But why?

"Want me to tell you something I found out just today?" Rob asked.

Logan gave him a big smile. "Absolutely."

"Don't encourage him," Sadie muttered.

"Let him speak. Go ahead, Rob."

With every eye on him, Rob said, "Once I talked with Dorn Alexander at the party, I knew something was screwy. Someone with as much success as she's had would have known about the people I mentioned. Anyway, I have some connections, so I made a few calls this morning. Guess what?"

"What?" Camille said, smiling.

"Dorn Alexander is thirty-eight years old and stands five feet nine inches."

Liz's heart pounded as everything fell into place. The discrepancy in Dorn's online appearance and how she actually looked. The difference in the quality of her writing. Francie had spelled it out in her story. The meanness of Donna and the surly behavior of Dorn. The yellow wig and the attacker's gray hair.

"Excuse me." Liz sprinted up the stairs, taking them two at a time. She flung open the door of the wardrobe in the Heirloom Room and grabbed the hatbox from the shelf. Inside was a plastic headstand. A few blonde hairs clung to it.

"Liz?" Logan said.

She turned to see the group had followed her.

"Rob, do you have a recent photo of Dorn Alexander on your phone?" Why had she not thought to do this earlier? But there'd been no reason to. She'd simply accepted that everyone at her inn was who they said they were. As had, apparently, the other writers in the group.

"I do." He pulled it up quickly and handed the phone to Liz.

She studied the image, which showed a woman dressed in fashionable clothes. She had long limbs and sleek locks of blonde hair.

"Caitlyn? When was the last time you saw the injured woman?" Liz asked.

"Right before I left the hospital. I peeked in on her in ICU."

"Look at this, will you? Look closely." Liz showed the screen to her friend.

Caitlyn did as she was asked, peering hard at the image. Recognition slipped across her features. "Wow!"

"All those photos she said were pictures of her taken years and years ago—they were the real Dorn all right, but not from as long ago as we were told. Now we know the identity of the woman in the hospital. And we know who put her there." Liz handed the phone back to Rob.

Sadie voiced the questions on everyone's minds. "But who is the fake Dorn? And where is she now?"

18

Chief Houghton stood at the front door of the Olde Mansion Inn, hat in hand, somberly eyeing those who lingered nearby looking at him.

"Thank you for this information." He lifted his notebook. "We have been aware of some of these facts, but your insights and suggestions are duly noted and will be investigated. With the footage from the security video and your own description of this woman, I'm confident we'll find her if she is still in the area. An impostor always slips up sooner or later." He started to step outside and turned back. "Rest assured we will be getting in touch with Mr. Alexander as soon as possible."

"Thank you so much, Chief."

"It's my job, Liz." His smile was warm.

"But what about Francie?" Sadie said.

"What about her?" he asked.

"Are you going after her? What if she did away with whoever's pretending to be Dorn? She and Francie could both be guilty."

He stared at Sadie for a moment, then dropped his gaze to the hat in his hand. A curious expression flickered across his features and disappeared as he lifted his head. Liz could swear she saw humor in his eyes.

"I appreciate your interest and your help, but there's no reason to go after Francie. But I can make sure she's okay and being taken care of." He clapped the hat on his head as he stepped outside. "I'll keep you updated."

"Oh, but—"

Logan caught Sadie's hand. "It'll be okay," he said softly.

"That's right, Sadie," Liz added. "We've done our best, and now we have to let the police do theirs."

Sadie wrinkled her nose as if she didn't approve of police working without her, but she said nothing else.

"Besides, we haven't had dinner yet." Logan looked at his watch. "Do you think the restaurant will still be open?"

"I doubt any place will be open this late, either here in Pleasant Creek or in Bertram," Liz said. "But there's plenty of food for all of us in the refrigerator for a potluck, if you're willing to have it."

"Sounds good to me!" Camille said. "I'm starved."

"So am I," Rob said. He glanced at Liz. "I'd like to stay. If you don't mind, that is."

Liz was nothing if not hospitable, and for once, she was grateful for Rob's nosiness. "Sure. Stay and have a late supper with us. I think Camille would like that," she added with a smile.

Camille blushed.

"Well, shucks. We're all dressed up to go somewhere swanky." Sadie sighed, fingering the fabric of her top.

"Then we'll use Liz's fancy china and take pictures," Mary Ann said. "Then you'll have something to remember about this day besides impostors who do horrible things."

"My camera takes great photos, Sadie," Rob said. "I'll take some shots worthy of being framed."

———— *//////////////////////////* ————

At two a.m., her well-fed guests having gone home hours ago, a sound roused Liz from sleep. She lay quietly, listening hard. When she heard nothing more, she closed her eyes and tried to go back to sleep.

Something hit the floor in the Heirloom Room above her. The

sound was soft, like a clothes hanger falling to the floor or a small ornament falling over on a table. She sat up and remained perfectly still, staring at the dark ceiling. Quiet, hurried, uneven footsteps walked back and forth.

Maybe Camille was up to her sleepwalking or snooping again.

Or maybe the Dorn impostor had returned for her things.

Liz slid out of bed, pulled on her robe, and put on her house slippers. The inn was quiet as she stole through the sitting room and up the stairs. She paused at the top, glancing around the landing and noting that no one was about. A thin band of light showed beneath the door of the Heirloom Room. As she approached, she heard the soft rustling sounds of movement.

How had she gotten in? Liz had locked up after everyone went home. Could she have been in the house the whole time, perhaps hiding out in one of the third-floor rooms while the dinner party was going on?

Liz stared at the door, fear rising in her throat. What if the impostor came after her again? She glanced around the hallway and grabbed the first thing that presented itself as a weapon—a small marble bookend from a nearby table. The books it had been supporting leaned sideways and crashed to the floor. A moment later, the door opened. Just a crack at first, then wider until Liz saw the woman with frizzy gray hair and a wild look in her eyes.

"Sneaking up on me, Liz?"

"No, I—"

"You can't stop me. None of the others have been able to stop me."

"Stop you?"

She sneered. "I'll show them all I'm a better writer, yes, I will. Miss Beauty Queen Camille will never live to see her books in the stores. And Jack Todd has solved his last case." She stepped out into the hallway, becoming a sinister, backlit shadow. Liz swallowed hard. She reached behind her, feeling along the wall until she found a light switch and turned it on. A soft golden light gently illuminated the area. She tightened her grip around the heavy bookend.

"The great Dorn Alexander won't rise from the ashes, no, she won't," the woman said. "Telling me my writing isn't good, then trying to leave me behind while she mingles with others. They wouldn't believe in my genius and talent, but Patrice Barnhill will be a star, you just wait and see. I'll knock them all down to size."

Patrice Barnhill? Liz searched her memory until she made the connection. That was the name of a writer the others had mentioned during a meeting. They had been glad of her absence. But apparently she had followed the real Dorn to Pleasant Creek and had taken over her identity. For a couple days, she'd gotten away with it.

Logan's door opened, and a moment later, so did Camille's.

"Y-you're Patrice, aren't you?" Liz asked, as much for Camille and Logan's benefit as her own.

The woman came nearer. Although she leaned heavily on her cane, she emanated danger. Liz's heart pounded.

"Of course I am!" she shouted. "Who else would I be?"

"We all thought you were Dorn—"

"She tried to steal my success, so I stole it back."

"What do you mean, Patrice?" Logan asked as he and Camille approached.

She turned her crazy gaze on him.

"You! You and Dorn thought you could destroy my career by telling me my writing was weak and flawed, that my characters were one-dimensional. I've known all along what you want."

"And what's that?" he asked quietly.

"You want to steal my ideas!" She raised her cane, and anyone seeing her would never believe she had any handicap at all unless it was the handicap of insanity.

"Dorn—I mean, Patrice, why don't we go downstairs and have a cup of tea and you can talk to us?" Liz figured this suggestion would meet with resistance, but she didn't expect the woman to turn and rush at her, wielding the cane like a club.

Liz threw the bookend, which missed its mark and fell harmlessly to the floor with a thud.

Both Logan and Camille took advantage of the distraction and pounced on Patrice, pinning her arms and subduing the crazed woman bent on revenge for some imagined slight.

With trembling hands, Liz retrieved her phone from her pocket and dialed 911. "It's Liz Eckardt at the Olde Mansion Inn." Her voice shook. "The person who assaulted the woman in the hospital is here. Send someone, and please hurry!"

Liz walked Logan and Camille to their cars late Sunday afternoon. Sadie and Mary Ann joined the small farewell party as the authors lingered a few more minutes.

"Liz," Logan said, taking one of her hands in both of his, "this place is so wonderful. I'd like to return one day, bring my laptop, and sit out in the gazebo to write."

"That would be wonderful. Please do."

"I wouldn't mind returning either," Camille said. "I'd like to see Rob again, and I'd like to pick your brain some more about happenings at the inn."

"You haven't had enough while you were here?" Liz laughed.

"Well, maybe for now. But you have a treasure trove of good stuff in your head for a writer to pick through."

"You'll be welcome anytime, Camille. I do have one question for you, though."

"What's that?"

"When you first went upstairs, you seemed very interested in the staircase and newel post where the real Dorn's blood had been, as if you knew what had happened there. Why was that?"

Camille shook her head. "I did? I don't remember doing that, but I love old houses, and I love architecture and design. Those were admiring glances, I'm sure. Or maybe it was writer's instinct, as if I knew subconsciously that it had a story to tell." She gave Liz a sharp look. "You didn't suspect I had anything to do with the assaults, did you?"

"Maybe, for a minute or two. I'm sorry." She offered an apologetic smile.

Camille grinned at her. "Under the circumstances, I would have felt the same way, so it's okay. I have to admit I was worried I'd been snatching things in my sleep after I found the wooden spoon the other morning, but I really think we can chalk that magpie behavior up to Francie's uniqueness."

"Camille knows a good investigator suspects everyone," Logan said fondly. "I suspected you for a little while, Liz. Until you got walloped in the head, that is."

Liz reached for her head, which was still tender. "I can honestly say I hope never to be hit with a cane again."

"Did you suspect me, Logan?" Sadie asked.

Logan turned to her. His expression was one of tender regard and a bit of sadness.

"Ah, my dear Sadie. No, never you." He brushed a curl of white hair from her forehead. "You have added beauty, fun, and joy to these last several days. As I've told you more than once, it's as if I have my beloved Betsy with me once more. You not only have her same smile, you have her same heart."

"Betsy?" Mary Ann and Liz echoed.

"I'm happy to have been your surrogate big sister for a few days." Sadie laid one hand against his cheek. "Anytime you need to talk, you have my phone number and e-mail address, and you know where I live."

"Absolutely."

A black sedan that looked like a rental pulled up and parked nearby, drawing everyone's attention. A tall, handsome man in khakis and a light jacket got out of the driver's side. He looked toward them, nodded, but said nothing as he went to the passenger door and opened it.

It took a little while for the passenger to get out. She was bruised and bandaged, and moved very slowly. Logan walked toward her.

"Dorn?" he asked.

Clinging to her companion's arm, she gave Logan a smile that obviously hurt her. "Hello, Logan. It's so good to see you at last." A Southern drawl threaded through her voice. "This is my husband, Billy."

As everyone congregated around her and greeted one another, Liz wanted to cry because Dorn had been through so much, just for being successful and in the wrong place at the wrong time.

"It's not everyone who has two such close calls and survives," Camille said. She reached out and touched the woman's shoulder tenderly. "How are you feeling?"

"Like I fell down a staircase and got stabbed the next day." Another pain-filled smile. "At least the doctors said there's no brain damage, so I don't have to worry about my career."

"Won't you come inside, Dorn, and have some refreshment?" Liz asked.

"Thanks, but we're flying out tonight. I need to get her home," Billy said. "The sooner we're there, the better she'll feel and the sooner she'll recover. The stab wound was superficial, thank goodness. And we've got excellent medical care arranged for her."

"I wanted to stop in case any of our group was still here. And to meet you, Liz. I feel like I owe all of you an explanation," Dorn said.

Liz smiled. "You don't owe us anything, after all you've been through."

"But you deserve to know the whole story. I miscalculated my travel time and arrived at your inn quite early Thursday morning. Patrice was with me."

"Are you kidding?" Camille screeched. "She came with you? She said online that she couldn't make it."

"Right. We live not too far away from each other, and she surprised me by showing up shortly before I left. The last months she has moaned and groaned about being unable to go, so of course I hadn't expected to have her with me on that trip, but she told me she'd gotten it worked out. I could hardly turn down her plea for a ride."

"You poor thing," Sadie said.

"Patrice was such a miserable companion that I drove faster than I intended. In fact, we drove straight through."

"My goodness, all the way from Louisiana?" Liz said. "That was a long trip!"

"And even longer when one is stuck in the car with someone badgering, baiting, and complaining without pause. At any rate, when we got here, I was so tired all I wanted was a shower and some sleep. The door was open and we went inside. We waited by the desk for a bit, but when it seemed no one knew we'd arrived, I went upstairs to try to find someone. Patrice slipped up there too—she can move rather well despite the limp—but I didn't know until I started to go back down and she spoke right behind me. I turned, she pushed, and . . . well, I tumbled head over heels all the way down. I didn't realize that by 'got it worked out,' she meant she was going to try to kill me and take my place."

"Why, that's horrible," Mary Ann said. "You could have broken your neck."

"But we're so glad you survived." Liz smiled at her. "You seem to be on your way to recovery, though it might take awhile."

"That's right," Sadie agreed, "but at least you answered some of the questions we've been asking each other."

"Good. I didn't want you all to wonder what had happened and how, because I doubt Patrice is going to be very forthcoming when questioned."

"She may be institutionalized for a while," Billy said. "The word I got was she had a complete psychotic breakdown."

"And we thought Francie was unwell," Camille said. She gave Dorn a warm smile. "I'm glad to know you are as good and kind as you seemed online."

"Thank you for saying that. I hate that Patrice decided to impersonate me and took my name but kept her own miserable personality." She laughed slightly, then winced and touched a bruise on her jaw. "Maybe she'll tell the police where she hid my purse, coat, and shoes. And I'm counting the moments until I can get to the salon and get my hair fixed. Patrice did a masterful job of disguising my real identity when she left me for dead."

Liz smiled sympathetically. She ran her own investigation back through her mind. "Billy, when you and I spoke on the phone, you said that Dorn had texted you several times. She couldn't have if she was in the hospital. I suppose Patrice had Dorn's phone and was able to figure out who you were from the contact list?"

Billy shook his head. "She fooled me, all right. I should have known it wasn't Dorn. The texts were pretty impersonal, now that I think about them, but I assumed she was just busy with the retreat." He turned to Dorn. "Honey, let's get you back in the car," Billy said. He looked at everyone. "We can't miss our flight. My brother will be back to retrieve Dorn's car at some point."

"Of course," Liz said. "Thank you so much for stopping by, and I hope to see you again sometime. Under better circumstances, of course."

"I believe Logan might organize another retreat here," Sadie said. She gave Logan a huge grin.

"That would be lovely," Dorn said. "Maybe I'll actually be able to attend this one."

Logan beamed at her. "Then we'll plan on it."

They watched until she was safely tucked in and comfortable. Billy bid them all goodbye, and they drove away.

As the others resumed their farewells, Sadie turned to Logan. "You make things right with Madison. If she loves you, she will forgive you."

"I'll certainly try. Thank you, Sadie, for listening to me and for drying my tears." He embraced her and kissed her forehead. "Don't forget me."

"As if I would, even if I could. And I may just keep writing." She stepped back.

"You'd better," Logan said. "I can't wait to find out what happens." He turned from Sadie and shook Mary Ann's hand. "It was so good to meet you. Take care of Sadie for me, will you? She's a special lady."

She laughed. "Sadie takes pretty good care of herself, but I'll keep an eye on her for you."

He turned to Liz and encased her hand in both of his. "Thank you for everything. Your inn is a beautiful place, and it has become very special to me." He squeezed her fingers warmly and let go. "Tell that friend of yours I might want to write a book about a mayor one day, and I'll be calling on him. He's quite a guy. But you already know that, don't you?"

She suddenly found she was holding back tears. It must have been the bright March sunshine. "Yes, I know that. And I'll deliver your message."

Logan looked at Camille. "Well, my dear young friend, I guess we'd better go our separate ways now. But we'll meet up again, soon I hope."

"Yes, we will. I like the idea of another retreat. Only next time, let's not have quite so much drama." She hugged each one in turn, giving her mentor a longer embrace. "Keep in touch."

With a last look at the inn, both authors made their ways to their cars. Liz sensed they both would have rather stayed a little longer, and she smiled. She would miss them too.

"Have a safe trip home," Sadie called out. "Both of you keep filling the world with your beautiful words."

"We'll do our best," Camille called back, waving goodbye. "If Liz will keep filling her house with interesting guests and fascinating stories."

Liz realized that the Olde Mansion Inn had seen plenty of each since she'd bought it and moved to Pleasant Creek. She turned to Mary Ann and Sadie, and smiled. Interesting guests and fascinating stories were all well and good, but she'd rather fill her home with good friends any day.

Learn more about Annie's fiction books at

AnniesFiction.com

We've designed the Annie's Fiction website especially for you!

Access your e-books • Read sample chapters • Manage your account

Choose from one of these great series:

Amish Inn Mysteries

Annie's Attic Mysteries

Annie's Mysteries Unraveled

Annie's Quilted Mysteries

Annie's Secrets of the Quilt

Antique Shop Mysteries

Chocolate Shoppe Mysteries

Creative Woman Mysteries

Hearts of Amish Country

Secrets of the Castleton Manor Library

Victorian Mansion Flower Shop Mysteries

What are you waiting for? Visit us now at **AnniesFiction.com!**